T0193532

THE INVERSE PROPORTION

NEW EDITION

LOUISE P N KIBUUKA

AuthorHouse™ UK
1663 Liberty Drive
Bloomington, IN 47403 USA
www.authorhouse.co.uk
UK TFN: 0800 0148641 (Toll Free inside the UK)
UK Local: 02036 956322 (+44 20 3695 6322 from outside the UK)

Because of the dynamic nature of the Internet, any web addresses or links contained in this book may have changed since publication and may no longer be valid. The views expressed in this work are solely those of the author and do not necessarily reflect the views of the publisher, and the publisher hereby disclaims any responsibility for them.

This book is printed on acid-free paper.

ISBN: 979-8-8230-8088-0 (sc)
ISBN: 979-8-8230-8087-3 (e)

Print information available on the last page.

Published by AuthorHouse   02/23/2023

authorHOUSE®

CONTENTS

DEDICATION

In memory of:

My best client and other fallen victims of the disease described in this book.

My lovely late grannies:
Ernest Kazinda
Julia Kidza Kiridde
Samalie Nakato
Salome Babirye;
Paulo Mawayira
Esther and Sedrulaka Katula

My love and grandmother of my children;
Cecelia Nakanwagi

ACKNOWLEDGEMENTS

My great appreciation to:

The children and grandchildren of my best client.

Thank you for being very supportive and caring for your Mum!

Many thanks to the Alzheimer's society (USA) for their unreserved kindness for sending me the News daily and allowing me to use the information in creating awareness of the disease. The compiled information, personal research and observations in this book are my contributions towards the fight against the plague of the 21st Century.

PREFACE

"Everyone with a brain must dread this plague of the 21ˢᵗ century!

More than five million (5,000,000) Americans are currently affected by one of the disease's conditions; five hundred thousand (500,000) people die each year from the incurable condition (January 14 -2015 Health Day news).In UK there are an estimated 900,000 people with dementia. The number is projected to rise to more than 1.6 million people by 2040.It is predicted, 209,600 people are likely to develop the illness in 2022,,that is one every three minutes.70 percent of people in care homes have dementia or severe memory problems. 19 July 2022 .https://www.alzheimers.org.uk.

'During 2000-2012 one condition of the disease killed more people than the dreaded Breast and Prostate cancer.' (alz.org).

Two-thirds (2/3) of the victims are women.

The reality of the disease is a mystery yet to be unfolded by modern science (A woman Nation video report, 15/3/2015).

Latest research results show that those whose walking pace begins to slow and who also have cognitive complaints are more likely to develop the disease within 12 years.(October 2016).

Medical researchers have revealed there are conclusions that Hypothyroidism is associated with increased risk of dementia. The association is influenced by comorbidity and age. Every 6 months of elevated TSH increased the risk of dementia by 12%, also the length of hypothyroidism influences the risk of dementia. (Med.ncbi.nlm.nih.gov.)

The book is a compilation of availed information, personal observation and research about the disease.

The author's account is a compendium to create awareness and understanding that the condition is an illness; to highlight the reality of the illness and the struggle to cope with it's stigma as the struggle to find the cure continues.

The characters in this book are fictional, are only used to highlight the reality of the condition.

The book is meant to create awareness of the need to care for the victims and the ardent need for the cure.

Louise P .N. Kibuuka

CHAPTER 1

Talk to Them While They Still Can!

It was a beautiful early morning on a Saturday. As I peeped through the nylon curtains of my front window, I could see the bright bulging white stony moon still up in the dark sky. There was only one star visible.

My eyes wondered to scan for more interesting scenery. The street was empty, only the street electric lights sparkled yellow lights through the green canopy of the Chester and Cherry trees that lined the streets. Even my usual early guests; the pair of Magi pies and the Red chest Robins were late for their favourite oats meal for breakfast. I decided to dive back under the blanket for a few minutes to warm up for the day!

"Thank God! It is summer at last!" "Best of all I got a new job!" I started the morning with an extended stretch of my fore limbs because of what I thought was good news!

I decided to visit my friend who lived a few meters from my house to break the good news of my new job.

"I know very little about illnesses of the elderly people, apart from the awareness course we attended at my place of work. I don't know what I am going to do with the lady." "I am worried to the spine!"

I explained to my friend, Joy, whom I trusted would be happy to

celebrate with me for the new job.

"Tell me more about your new job!" My friend inquired with curiosity.

"A new client, I have to care for at the Good Samaritan De-me-ntia

Centre." I replied stressing the last two words.

"Oh my goodness! The disease is horrible! You better ask them for a different client!" "You will not be able to tell her anything, how about if she runs into the road and she is knocked down by a car!"

She exclaimed, with disapproval

"Oh! No! No! Please, stop!" I hysterically protested. "It is the disease condition which is bad, not the person! I am there to help stop the disease taking over her life! I want her to live a better life than what she is experiencing. I have met the lady; she is a very pleasant woman." I politely continued to-explain.

"Oh? What? Pleasant with dementia illness?" "You are mistaken; those people with dementia are mad people!" My friend insisted.

"I admit, I do not know much about the disease, I guess even you don't know much about the disease but you are stereo-typing." "It can happen to anybody. I have done some research; currently one in three of those above 65 is likely to get the disease." "Supposing it was you and people left you to yourself!" "Besides... aging is a universal and natural phenomenon!" I was still explaining and my friend took over....

"How much do you know about the diseases which affect the old people? May be it is that new disease -it is infectious! You might get it and then spread it to us!" Joy continued.

I could feel I was becoming uneasy over her opinions and speculations about the disease. I felt it was time to leave.

"I will find out, I know it is not infectious, but I hear it can be inherited!" "I will see you later! Have a nice day!" I said to her as I rose to leave.

"I admit I don't know anything about the disease; part of my mission is to find out about it; understand more about the disease by looking after somebody who is suffering from the disease." I, mumbled to myself as I hurried back to my house.

I decided to get to the office early the next morning to search for more information from my supervisor and to find out more about my new client before I could meet her the next day.

In the afternoon I visited the local library run by the Council, where internet and books were free. I opened and perused through several websites displaying information about dementia illness, aging conditions and memory loss. By the time I got what I needed my eyes had rusted from the brightening screen; I felt my head was bigger, heavy and confused. Armed with a few scribbled notes from what I had found, I decided to borrow some books and I left for home.

There was a lot of information about the disease, but I was disappointed to find that there was no cure yet for the disease.

Later in the evening after my dinner of sweet potatoes, spinach and a steamed pork belly slice; I read through my notes I had found earlier that day:

'It is a mystical disease that robs people of their brain cells; mainly the aging people; although the condition could also start at an earlier age.' The notes struck me like a bomb.

Another piece indicated the disease was heritable..

'The advice is: What they need is assurance and hope. Talk to them while they still can.'

It all sounded very sad and disappointing!

"What was she like before she became ill?" I wondered!

The next day I woke up early to find the famous Samaritans Care

Centre which was located in the South Eastern part of London.

Although the location was not too far from where I lived, it was rather in a secluded place hard to find, located in the center of a huge green village situated very near a railway station.

The bus route that went to the place made several turns before it got to the place. I feared I would not be able to get to the place on time. I didn't want to be late, so I decided to wake up earlier than usual and instead of going by bus I decided to walk. This would save a few pounds off the transport fee too.

I took a short cut through a dog walk park; I had to keep a keen eye on the ground, in case I trailed in dogs' pooh.

"Sometimes dog owners are not fair to others who do not keep dogs. The dog owners are simply not keen to clean up their dogs' mess! "I am happy I didn't step in it!" I complained as I trekked through the thick green grass that was covered with the morning dew.

As I opened the black painted Iron Gate, to squeeze through, my spirit resisted a little, for the path looked deserted and lonely too. After moments of still ponder, I regained confidence and managed to squeeze through and got to the other side of the gate.

A fresh cold breeze swept across my unsheltered face. It was a new micro climate created by the woodland!

Soon I realised I was alone through a lonely path through the woodland.

The leaves were all green. The air smelt fresh and felt cool; there was a sweet fresh sensation that was created by a variety of trees: Cherry, British oak, Pine trees and many more. I stole a moment, stood to admire the picturesque landscape of the green land and its natural beauty.

Then I realised it was stupid to enjoy the woodland, I would be late for work. I checked my Nokia phone for the first time. It was five minutes to clock nine- The reporting time.

My Nokia had once been nicknamed a 'dinosaur' by a colleague in the office due to its advanced model, but it was still good enough to tell the correct time. I chocked a light laughter at the reflection.

Trotting like a hare, over and down the bridge that was sheltering and overhanging over the railway station, I could hear down below the speeding train struggling to engage its breaks for it had reached the Good Samaritan's station.

Instantly a frightened Red Chest Robin flew across in front of my face, almost knocking me over! Then the bird quickly escaped into the bush.

"Hoops! The robin!" I exclaimed and dashed on.

The lonely path through the wood. Photo by the author.

I hurried across through to the main street that led to the iron guarded building- The Good Samaritan's House. There were two glass doors that led into the building. Both were closed. I surveyed the first one, there was no bell to ring, and then I went to the second one; there were several glass buttons to be pressed and lastly I saw what seemed to be the reception bell. I must have guessed right, for when I pressed the sunken notch, I heard a noisy cracking sound and the door clicked open. I immediately rushed in.

"Good morning!" I politely greeted the lady who stood by the Reception

Desk..

"Good morning!" "Are you visiting somebody?" A well-body built lady answered my greeting with a smile and a query as she welcomed me.

"Oh, not really, my name is Justina; I have been seconded to this Centre to take care of one of your clients!" I answered as I flushed my identification Card.

"You are welcome, Justina, just go through that door through that corridor; you will find another entrance into a big hall, that is the Centre, I am sure the manager is expecting you!" Th lady explained as she ushered me through the door.

"Thank you!" I tip toed to reach the handle for the door, grubbed it to lower it down, but the door did not open!

"Sorry, we have to put safety locks to keep the clients safe", the lady said as she pressed a secrete button that pushed the door open. I cautiously walked through the door through to a long corridor enclosed by white walls plastered with several murals and notices. Soon I arrived at another glass door that led into the hall.

I knocked at the door and somebody from inside shouted a 'come in please'. I pushed the door open and I introduced myself to a smartly dressed lady I expected to be the manager, who was seated behind a computer.

"Glad to meet you Justina, my name is Miss Panessa. The manager of the Centre". She responded.

"Are you here for Kevinah? She will be here in a moment; I always come in earlier to prepare my plans for the day before everybody comes in. It gets very busy in here. Wait and see what happens! I am not trying to scare you off your new job, though! I need help with that lady; she wonders around and puts things in her mouth. Your duty is to protect her, follow her everywhere and see that she does not put things in her mouth! And now if you will excuse me, just find a seat and I will get back to you in a moment!" She charted on, instructed and got back on to the computer.

Before turning to find a seat, my emotion betrayed me and I murmured something: "This is my induction in brief."

Miss Pannesa raised her beautiful round eyes over her silver lined spectacles, gazed at me, temporarily stopping her typing.

Feeling embarrassment, fearing Miss Panessa might have noted my

misjudgment. I instantly created something to say:

"Can I have her file please? I can read through as I wait". I asked audibly.

"I will find it for you in a moment," answered Miss Panessa and she resumed her typing.

I took a seat as instructed and my eyes began to wander through the massive hall. It was a well-ventilated room with large glazed glass windows and doors overlooking a beautiful garden on both right and left sides of the hall. The furniture included comfortable wooden chairs with comfortable cushions, wooden tables, a few bookshelves and cupboards. On one of the tables was an Indoor football pitch.

A very large flat screen television set stood on a glass stand at one corner and next to it was a wide and high wooden shelf packed with music compact Discs (CDs) and Digital Video DVDs packages nicely displayed.

There were other structures too: two dolls lay in a mini baby plum, packs of indoor puzzle boxes, hand balls, a pack of laundry kits, old clothing and knitting wool in one corner. There was an old structure of a Victorian Organ displaying a dusty surface, indicating it had not been used for a very long time.

At another far corner was a big dustbin, a trolley, a fridge, a long high shelf with nicely displayed ornamental plates below which was attached a cupboard for storing cutlery.

It was a while before my host, Miss Panessa, found time to hand me the file I had asked for.

My first instinct was to find out the history of my client:

Kevinah had been a housewife, a mother of six; once busy with house work chores; cleaning, ironing, cooking, gardening and escorting children to school. She worked in schools and a hospital as a support worker.

Her birth date indicated she was now an octogenarian. She preferred having traditional dishes and no sugar was to be added in her tea.

Her ex-husband was a company director, who demanded smartly pressed suits and starched white collar shirts. The black shoes needed a shine too. The wife had to line up clean socks and washed dirty ones every day. His dinner was expected to be on time to give him time to digest it before he retired to bed. His breakfast was to be served on dot at seven. He always had toast, butter, baked beans, poached egg and bacon, followed by a cup of strong coffee with three sugars. His desert was always a puff of Cuban Cigar after every meal.

When he felt had had too much on his plate, he absconded duty, both at home and at work. It was six years after settling down in a new country, when he remembered he had a wife before called, Kevinah. He decided to call and ask how their six children were fairing.

Kevinah was no fool; she had sensed changes in her husband long before he eloped with a young model. She had found herself a cleaning job

in a school where she used to take her children. After six months of toiling as a cleaner, she got a second job as a kitchen assistant in a nearby hospital. All this combined with household chores bore such a heavy burden not only on her body but an extra strain on her brain. A few years later she found herself on a hospital bed in the very hospital where she worked.

Later on during my work at the Good Samaritan Centre, I came to learn that another client by the name Nicky had been hospitalised in the same ward with Kevinah in the same hospital. Nicky had had persistent quarrels with her husband for several years. One fateful day, the couple had a fierce fight that left Nicky for the dead. She was later diagnosed with a serious brain injury.

Those were just two members of the group of an average of fourteen men and women who were daily attendants at the Good Samaritan Centre, Each of the members had a unique condition of the disease, but shared one common symptom: they always seemed confused and forgetful.

CHAPTER 2

The Reality of the Disease

You will never understand the reality of the situation until you really get involved in it. My first months at the Centre were full of challenging and interesting adventures.

Each day seemed different. Clients behaved differently, each day! One would do something the right way one minute, but did exactly the opposite the next minute. Tearing me to pieces!

I could feel the agony, my client was going through. I tried to imagine what was going on in her mind and why most of the clients behaved in such weird ways!

From what I had read about the condition and what I was observing among the clients at the Centre; especially my new client, was quite frightening. I wished I would never grow old. I remembered, growing was a natural phenomenon, and not only the old people suffered from the disease conditions. I tried to imagine what was taking place in each of the clients' brain to behave the way they were behaving.. Most of them behaved like nursery school children. They had to be reminded to go to the lavatory; they would say they had lost their handbags when they had the bags strapped on their hands. Others would ask why they were at the Centre at that time instead of being in their homes!

I remembered a picture I had taken at the Entebbe Airport while on holiday to my home country, Uganda in Africa. I had admired a flock of noisy yellow weaver birds that seemed to welcome us to the land of sunshine, greeting the visitors as they sung noisily. Later I noted the noisy birds were selfishly harvesting palm tree leaves to build nests for their young. They had no clue they were destroying the very tree on which they perched to construct their nests! They kept picking the palm leaves, tearing them into smaller pieces; weaving them into clusters of straw to form basket nests for their young flock. The devoured palm tree stump was left hanging on for life.

At a distance the picture resembled that of the destroyed brain cells I had read about in my research about the disease that had affected my client that had perhaps destroyed her brain with the toxic plaques.

It was my second day at the Centre. Kevinah was already in the hall when I came in. She regarded me with unreserved suspicion, as if I had come to steal her belongings!

She kept putting all things away at a corner in the hall: papers, clothing, and books.

She seemed not to bother herself about whom I was or why I was there.

She simply went on with her work as if it were her daily duties. When she finished hiding all her wealth, she looked around and pushed a chair so that she could sit down. She sat down steadied herself comfortably and looked across the room; she apparently had forgotten all about me.

There were other clients seated in a group in one corner of the room watching television and some reading newspapers.

After a long while, she turned to me and asked, "What have you come for?"

"I came to see you again! "I replied.

"See me?" "Ok!"....blurrrrrrrrrrrr... Here blurrr... she lost words as she tried to answer and murmured something pointing at a chair next to her. I guessed she was probably asking me to sit down.

I smiled and moved nearer to her. As I drew closer Kevinah smiled too

and pointed to the chair next to her and she clearly said:

"Sit down!" I pulled the chair and sat down and I said, "Thank you!" I was trying to work out what to say to her, then one of the Centre staff, by the name Liz, came in through the double glass door entrance into the

Hall pushing a trolley carrying several white tea cups, three teapots, a two liters plastic bottle of milk, a glass bowl of sugar and a small white bottle of sweetener. White side-plates and several white saucers, obviously to match the tea cups. On the lower shelf of the trolley were an empty green bucket and a biscuit tin.

"I have not had anything to eat since morning!" Pricilla, one of the lady clients, among the group, on seeing the trolley complained. The cups cluttered and rattled and the noise grew louder as the trolley was pushed along the narrow passageway through the hall to where a group of clients were seated watching television..

"That isn't true, Pricilla, I had just served you a cup of tea when the others came in." Liz, the lady staff pushing the trolley, answered.

"No! You didn't! I have had nothing to eat since yesterday!" Pricilla insisted.

"Do not worry; there is enough tea for everyone." Liz addressed her softly.

Pricilla displayed a guilty smile. She seemed very happy she was getting something to eat at last!

I felt sorry for Pricilla, I imagined she must have been very hungry, perhaps she lived alone and there had been no one to give her breakfast. Then I realised I had to get acquainted with my client; I turned to talk to Kevinah.

"Do you remember me Kevinah? I was with you yesterday! Shall we join our friends for a cup of tea?"

"Wetina"! (Meaning No!) Kevinah, resisted my request," I don't want to go I say!" She was getting agitated.

"I did not mean to offend you! I just wanted us to move nearer to the ladies so that we can share a cup of tea!" I tried to persuade her.

"Tea?" Kevinah asked with a smile. "Yes, a cup of nice hot tea!" I answered.

Kevinah quickly got up and we transferred ourselves to join the other clients who had by then doubled in number.

I should have first mentioned the word 'tea'; it seemed a magic word to broker the friendship.

While Kevinah enjoyed a cup of tea and a couple of biscuits, I overheard another lady client from the group asking her neighbour:

"Do I live here?" she asked the lady seated next to her. Apparently, both ladies seemed to be of the same age.

"She's definitely gone insane! She is only sixty- five and she can't remember where she lives!" A male client who sat a few meters away from the ladies, overheard the conversation, and cross-referenced to her; broke into laughter, annoyingly bunging his walking stick on the floor.

"You don't live here Miss! We only come here to have tea, biscuits, fish and chips!" the male client teased loudly, thumping his feet loudly and banging his walking stick on the tiled floor again.

"Don't be rude, I only asked and mark your words Mr.," "I am not a Miss! I am Mrs. Webster!" The lady client retaliated.

Realising the heated debate may not end, Janet, another staff who was standing by; intervened by presenting an activity:

"Today, we are going to talk about our school days!" She introduced the subject.

Janet had just come in with charts and a box full of toys,

A male staff member by the name, Joseph cleared away the cups and pushed the trolley back to the kitchen grumbling on his way out of the hall.

"I am not feeling well today! I hate this place! I wish I could get another job!" He grumbled quietly as he pushed the trolley full of dirty cups out of the hall.

"Bernard, do you remember your school days?" Janet continued, addressing the male client in the group who had confronted the lady who sought to know whether she lived in the hall.

"Oh! Yes! We wore army green kirk shorts; long socks and very heavy black boots! You had to polish the shoes every morning, otherwise, the headmaster would pull you out of the assembly queues and ask you to polish his shoes too! It was very intimidating and embarrassing too!" Bernard paused to clear his voice..."ehhe!" and then..."Especially in front of the girls!" Bernard recounted in a croaking broken voice.

Everybody burst into laughter!

"How about you, Jackleen?" Janet selected another elderly lady client,who was wiping her nose and applying red lipstick on her lips, keenly looking through a small Victorian mirror she had fished from an old grey wrinkled designer handbag.

"Oh! It was hard time," Jackleen, answered slowly in a coarse voice, still applying the lipstick. "Our mum had to wake us up before six O'clock in the wee hours of the morning in order to get us ready for school. We would have hardly had our breakfast than when she led us out of the house to start our trek!" Jackleen, recounted to a lingering laughter from other clients.

Everything seemed going on all right, everybody happy and participating. It seemed most of the clients remembered their past and were able to talk about historical events. 'How come then they were there in this Centre?' I wondered.

Suddenly, one of the clients appeared; she had just returned from the

Ladies' room:

"That is my chair, I was sitting there!" she shouted pointing to a chair which another elderly lady client was sitting.

"Leave me alone! I have been sitting here the whole day!" the victim tried to defend herself!

"No! I was sitting there before I went to the toilet!" Retorted her attacker.

Everyone's attention was distracted! Janet moved nearer to the distressed ladies to settle their seat dispute.

I watched the drama in disbelief. It was a hot argument.

I turned to find out how Kevinah was reacting to the situation, only to discover she was not in her seat! She was walking slowly behind other ladies' chairs brushing off dirt. Those seated on the chairs did not enjoy what Kevinah was doing! Eleanor, one of the quick tempered clients reacted openly shouting at her.

"Back off! What are you doing at the back of my chair?" she sounded very agitated.

Kevinah had slipped off when I was engrossed in listening to the reminiscent activities. She never sat in one place for long. She had to do something. She had been a very busy lady before she became ill. She liked cleaning up and making order. She most times played with the dolls, which she cared for like her real babies. She would talk to them, discipline, feed and dress them up.

Kevinah was very cultured, respectful of others. She was polite and never fought or quarreled with any one. When shouted at she would just go away, although at times when she felt, she didn't like one's comment, she would stand still and say: "I don't care!"

Kevinah was oblivious of the protests against her dusting of the chairs. She continued brushing and dusting as if it was her job.

"Alright, Eleanor, she is only helping clean the chairs; she is not going to hurt you!" I addressed Eleanor.

I felt it was my responsibility to arrest the situation. I walked over to Kevinah and I whispered to her.

"Let's go to see our babies!"

Kevinah nodded affirmatively with a smile and we walked happily away from the rest of the group to play with the dolls in the min plum.

After the reminiscence activity, I learnt that Bernard, the man who had rudely reproached the lady, who wanted to know whether she lived at the Centre earlier; was a former professor in music at one of the leading Universities in London and was a new comer to the Centre.

I realised too, when I talked to Kevinah in a low voice or whisper, it seemed to calm her down and would draw her attention. She would stop what she was doing and would come closer to me; smile and try to start a conversation. Unfortunately she had lost most of her verbal ability to construct complete sentences.

The loss of her ability to engage in conversation with me was very disappointing for both of us. Kevinah seemed to have been a sociable lady in her good days. She had a sweet smile most times when she felt well. I could see that she had lots of stories to tell me, and I wanted to know her more and most of all how she was feeling. I felt pity for her. Sometimes, I was crossing my professional boundaries. Kevinah was amazingly friendly the moments she felt well. She could show that I was her best friend. She reminded me of my own grandmother, who was very friendly to almost everybody. She would touch the middle part of her chest, with both hands enclosing her heart to express something she deeply felt.

CHAPTER 3

It's a Person-Centered Approach

It was my third day at the Good Samaritan's Centre, clients were talking to each other and some seemed to speak in foreign languages; others

could not understand what others were saying; but everybody had something to say ;so they talked to each other; laughing; somehow they all seemed to understand and enjoy each other's company. That's what mattered. Some did share genuine conversations; some clients seemed to have permanent friends and they always sat together; others colonised special seats and would never accept to sit anywhere else.

At a distance the conversations sounded likes voices heard during the Redeemed Pentecostal Church services; each one of the faithful believers praying and yearning for a different gift from the Holy Spirit.

As I sat in the staff room to have my break during lunchtime break; I pondered over what the different clients had talked about the previous day during the reminiscence activity about the clients' school days.

Some could remember very well what they did long time ago; but others would not say anything. Kevinah, my client, had not said anything.

'Does this mean each one of them was at a different stage of the course of the disease or does the disease affect each person differently?' I pondered. I decided my next assignment would be to study the course of the disease, the duration of each stage and what the symptoms were. One other important duty was to try helping Kevinah get more involved in activities with other clients or make her stay longer with the group, perhaps she would be able to remember some words and talk about her past.

Kevinah, loved to play with dolls. She cared for the dolls like real children. She would talk to them and sometimes would talk to some staff members as if they were her children too; but would say only one word or two.

"Are you ok?", "Me know". Sometimes when angry would say more words like, "I don't want to know!"

Several months later, I was still working at the Centre, I had by then

become a great friend of Kevinah. I had made other friends too.

Although, I was a one-to one for Kevinah, I found it was very difficult not to talk to other clients. I tried to learn my boundaries, but I had this conviction that all staff working with clients under the same roof had a duty to work as a team .Very often I crossed the boundaries and broke the rules!

"After all we all have the same goal: to safeguard and keep our clients happy in their final days!" I would excuse myself.

Kevinah had become very used to me; a few other clients too, would freely talk with me. Miss Panessa was very much pleased that Kevinah seemed happy with me, but she never forgot reminding me of my main duties and boundaries.

"Keep to your client, Justina, I don't want you to get into trouble with Social Services, they pay you to look after only her!" She would redirect whenever I digressed from my boundaries.

Kevinah loved walks. Every morning, after she had had a few rounds of inspections in the hall; I would take her for a walk in the building. During good sunny warm weather we would walk outside in the garden, we would sit on a bench in the garden and I would tell her stories about my children. She seemed to understand all what I was saying! She would laugh and try to comment, in a word or two.

She would then try to tell me stories in a few broken words; sometimes she would use gestures, mostly touching her heart…"You see I told him I couldn't do it". She repeatedly would say the same sentence most of the time.

This worried me lots, thinking somebody might have once tried to

harm her, or was she always remembering her husband but could not tell

the whole story?

Afternoons were more relaxed. Most clients took a nap after a heavy

lunch. But sometimes, when it was hot there were incidents.

It was three o'clock one afternoon. Kevinah was having a nap. Some of other group members were asleep too, some snoring loudly in their seats, others were awake talking to each other.

June one of the clients suddenly stood up, picked her handbag and appeared as if she was leaving for home. It was not yet time for clients to be dropped home.

Seeing no other staff around, I broke the rules of bounds and asked the lady what she was up to, and she answered:

"I am going to get my children from school" she answered grabbing her walking stick and securing her handbag in another hand as she hurried passed me.

"Someone has gone to collect them, don't worry," I cheated her.

"Is that so? And who must that be?" June stood still, holding her chin with her right hand, .She appeared thoughtful and suspicious.

"Perhaps your son!" I uttered without thinking!

"Oh! No! I don't have a son, may be my neighbour!" she corrected.

Embarrassed I didn't have the right answer for June, I decided to

initiate a nice chat.

"By the way, that's really a nice handbag! Where did you buy it? Marks and Spencer, I presume!"

"Oh! No! It was a gift from my husband on our second wedding anniversary!" "I only take it out on special occasions!" narrated June. She stood for a while, as if trying to remember something.

"So it must be another anniversary today!" I amused.

Remembering the magic word of 'a cup of tea' I tried to use it to calm June down.

"May be you could sit down while I find out who can serve us a cup of tea." I was restorative.

She reluctantly decided to find a seat and eventually sat down.

I was relieved to have succeeded make June forget her presumption to

get her children home and she sat down.

Miss Panessa, who was watching us from a distance, was not happy that I had not apprehended her repeated instructions of not attending to other clients. She apparently regarded it as an act of insubordination that I ignored her warnings. She felt it was high time to formally report me to the manager of the Institution and she sent a formal complaint to my agency.

"Can you please come and see me, Justina!" Miss Panessa beckoned me.

Asking June to excuse me for a moment, I rushed to answer Miss Panessa's call.

"Excuse me, I have to attend to somebody, will come back to you as soon as I am finished with her." I politely explained to June.

"Mind as you go!" June politely released me.

"Thank you!" I responded with a bow and rushed to meet Miss Panessa.

"You better stick to your duties, you are a 'one to one', and you must never leave your client for others." "This is the last warning to you! I will send a report to Social Services as well as to your Agency if you keep ignoring my instructions", she cautioned me.

"I am sorry, but the lady needed attention and there was no other staff to attend to her!" I apologized at the same time stubbornly objected; but Miss Panessa would not let me off the hook!

"While I work from here, I watch all the clients and oversee the staff, you inclusive!" "We are understaffed, and as you will realise later, some of my staff prefer talking to themselves other than attend to clients, I have to be on my heels all the time." "The other clients are none of your business, you understand?"

Miss Panessa was authoritative. Forcing a smile to sound polite to me while her eyes surveyed over the group of clients seated across, she summarily reprimanded:

"Remember, your duty is to care for Kevinah, not any other, understand?"

When she was finished with me, I proceeded to find Kevinah where I had left her sleeping. To my surprise, her seat was empty! She had walked out of the hall while I was busy talking with the manager, Miss Panessa. None of us saw her leave!

She had walked out of the hall and gone for a walk along the main corridor ,found a seat near the reception desk and sat down there conversing with whoever passed by.

When Kevinah got used to me she became very attached to me. We became inseparable. Kevinah always looked for me whenever I left her to have break or went to the ladies room without her.

I had to let her know where I was going and had to ask her to wait for me otherwise she would get up and follow me whenever I stood up to go somewhere; although at times, Kevinah would just want to go her way. I would then get a rude encounter when I tried to follow her!

"Why are you following me for?" Kevinah would rebuke me.

When she learnt to wait for me, her eyes would keep surveying the surroundings to check whether I was back.

On seeing me she would say" Are you back?" Sometimes she would just smile and give me an appreciative node.

Kevinah's responses most times were very pleasant and I became very fond of her.

Although, Kevinah could not say my name, I could see that she knew who I was, and if anybody mentioned the name Justina, one would notice a reaction in Kevinah: a smile or a turn round of her head in search of me. To me the reaction was very satisfying, that she was still cautious of her surroundings and she could recognise who was who, although she could not say the name. She was still an intelligent lady that she was before. We would hold hands and go for walks in the building or outside in the garden. For me she was Kevinah, my friend, not a disease-victim. Eventually I learnt to guess how she was feeling according to her reactions or most times I could guess what stage of the course of the disease she was in; early or advanced stage.

CHAPTER 4

Everybody Deserves A Break

One nice afternoon, after a good lunch, we played nice music of the sixties: Don Williams, Ricky Nelson, Dolly Patton, Elvis Presley and most of the clients were dancing and enjoying the afternoon. Most of the men clients were playing Dominos; others just sat listening to music. Some of the staff danced with the clients. Kevinah danced only a few times and she went to sit down. I continued to dance, while occasionally checked on her. Suddenly after a few swings with another client, I turned to check on my client, I did not see her! She had disappeared.

I rushed out in panic, out of the hall into the corridors, the toilets, as far as the smoking room to find Kevinah; but she was nowhere to be seen.

I decided to check the staffroom, Kevinah wasn't there! For a while, I stood lost, but did not wish to ask anybody for help in case they reported me to Miss Panessa. 'Where would she be? How would she open the doors to escape?' I could not think of any place where, Kevinah could have gone to!

Casting a glance through the window into the garden, there she was, comfortably strolling in the garden picking flowers sniffing at each bloom as she picked them.

I wasn't going to take more chances. Like a lunatic, I dashed out of the staffroom; through the corridor, into the hall where we both had sat before. Jumping past other clients dancing and some seated while others were clinging to their seats; I headed for the doors that led to the outside into the garden to meet Kevinah.

It took me a while fidgeting with the door locks to find which door opened to the outside to get into the garden.

'How on earth did she manage to get out into the garden?' I wondered.

By the time I got to the garden I was fully exhausted. My whole body was twitching and aching; my heart heavily pounding.

I stood still, held my breath for moments to prepare what to say to Kevinah. Suddenly came the familiar voice:

"I hope she has not put any of them flowers in her mouth!" It was Miss Panessa.

'Better to ignore her!' I murmured to myself and I continued to towards Kevinah.

As I approached her, I got a surprising well-come, "What are you following me for?" Kevinah asked.

For a moment, I was perplexed! Kevinah's question was smarter than

I expected!

Quite in context with the situation; and a complete sentence!

"It is a bit too hot to walk outside, let's get inside and put those beautiful flowers in a verse and then we shall have a cold drink of water!" I had to design a convincing answer.

Kevinah flushed a smile agreed to abandon her mission, left the garden; but escaped with a handful loot of bloom.

When we got inside the hall, I found an empty porcine vase and slotted the flowers into it. Placing the clay vase on one of the tables by the window I rushed to the staffroom to collect cold water from the fridge. Filled two glasses with cold drinking water and went back to the hall to find Kevinah.

I found her arranging some chairs. I was happy she was preparing a place for us to sit.

To my astonishment when I asked her to sit down she resisted and simply walked away, found a seat in another corner and sat down.

"Let her sit where she prefers and follow her all the time where she goes." Miss Panessa who watching us from her desk instructed.

I followed obediently like a sheep to where Kevinah was seated and handed her one of the glasses of water.

"Thank you!" Kevinah politely acknowledged.

"Oh! My God! What a job to do! I still have more hours to complete the day's swift" I exclaimed feeling already exhausted with my new job. My client puzzled me. At times she seemed to know her way out, what she wanted, and could find the right words to say when she chose to! That was contrary to what I had been told by the other staff-about symptoms of the disease.

While I was still in consultation with my mind about the reactions of my client; Janet one of the staff members brought in some indoor games equipment for activities. This time a bundle of inflated coloured plastic rings and an inflated plastic bag with protruding plastic fingers- an indoor game made purposely for entertaining and giving exercises to the elderly.

Everyone was very excited. The clients started playing like children, romping about, throwing about the brightly coloured plastic rings. When one hit the target, others clapped in applause.

One male member, Henry, however, was still busy dancing to some music of the sixties that played from the old music player system. He apparently seemed very happy. On seeing the rings, he picked three of them to the others' delight and they applauded loudly and happily clapping their hands.

"Go! Go! Henry! It is your turn!" they praised him.

Henry seemed very happy with the support he received from the members. He moved nearer to the music system and began to dance more rigorously. Instead of throwing the rings, he decided to wear them --one by one he slipped them on; over the head, over shoulders and suspended the three of them down around his waist!

"Look! What's he doing? How are you going to put them off? We told you to throw them rings!" One lady client angrily shouted to correct him.

"Oh? Then I will throw them rings!" Henry, innocently replied but continued to dance vigorously with the rings around his waist; dancing and matching well to the tune of the music, waving his hands to conduct the music as he danced. He appeared fully engrossed in the dance and enjoying it!

It took quite a while for Janet to convince Henry accept to remove the three damn rings off.

While I was admiring Henry I did not see Kevinah take off and disappear!

I decided to ask a lady client who was seated next where Kevinah had been sitting whether she had seen Kevinah go.

"I haven't seen her for years!" She answered. "But she was here a few minutes ago!" I insisted.

"Well look for her then, why ask me? Am I her keeper?" she snapped. I realised, I was proving a nuisance asking the wrong person.

I decided to talk with Janet instead.

"She wonders about lots when she feels like, probably she could be in the corridor; sometimes she may pick some things and put in her mouth, I bet that's why she needs a 'one to one'! Don't get me wrong, Hope I am not scaring you off! She is quite a troubled but a nice person." she rapped.

"Yes, I was told all that by the manager that I must follow her wherever she goes, but she seems quite elusive-very difficult to catch up with! I must find her!"

I was becoming angry and impatient, so I decided to cut the story Short.

I had to find my client again.

I rushed out of the hall, searched the corridors, the toilets, staffroom, and looked through the windows to check whether Kevinah was in the garden but she wasn't!

Failing to find her, returned to the hall to get more assistance from Janet.

"I did not find her!" I complained.

"Don't worry, we shall find her, all doors leading outside are permanently locked unless she went out when a visitor came in; ha! Ha!" Janet started laughing.

I felt very disappointed with Janet.

"It is no laughing matter! I've got to find her!" I snapped.

Janet, sensed I wasn't happy, she then suggested we check the smoking room that lay adjacent to the hall.

I rushed out to find the suggested room. Kevinah was seated comfortably, asleep.

"There you are!" I uttered, raising my hands in great relief!

Although, Kevinah, seemed to be asleep, she managed to show she had heard my movement. She tilted her head and tried to open her heavy eyelids; blinking twice before she finally managed to open her eyes. She frowned and rudely asked the intruder-me:

"What have you come in for?" Then she dropped her head and she fell back into her slumber again.

"You are my best friend! That's why I came to find you!" I whispered.

But Kevinah was not ready to wake up; she didn't reply.

She later struggled to open her eyes again. But her eyelids seemed heavier than before. She was soon back in her sleep again.

"She might have searched for a quiet place to have a nap." "Sometimes one needs a break" I talked to my self.

It was just the two of us. There was nobody else in the room It was quiet and calm. That's what Kevinah needed at that time, but she couldn't say it. This was a room used for smoking. Although the air in there was filthy, polluted and smelly, the atmosphere was quiet and still. I decided to empty the ash trays, opened the windows to let in some cool fresh breeze; then allowed my client to rest for a while. We still had sometime for her to rest before going home. I would have taken her for a walk or led her to her favourite activity to play with her dolls as usual; but this time, Kevinah, just needed a quiet place to sleep. She must have felt she needed a break and she had acted rightfully, she made her choice! I quite accepted that and I left her to sleep until it was time to take her home.

The following months I continued to study Kevinah's preferences. I learnt to give her choices and let her choose what suited her most, although sometimes I would make some changes to her choice to safeguard her from imminent danger. The practices restored Kevinah's confidence and she became very actively involved in many activities. She could walk through a group of clients with confidence. She would engage in activities without fear despite other clients' reproaches and protests. She would join and sit with the group, listen to music and watch the others dance. Sometimes she would accept to join in the dancing with the group, although this was very rare! She preferred to dance on her own while sitting on the chair. She was free to go anywhere she preferred, but I strictly had to follow her wherever she decided to go but I was never in her way unless it was very necessary for her safety. Kevinah's most troubled time was after a heavy lunch when she fancied to sleep and was not allowed to rest. She would become very agitated and very difficult, stubbornly refusing to do anything she was asked to do! I remember her refusing to wear her coat, at the Centre when it was time to go home. She resisted by folding her arms tightly making it very difficult to slip the coat on and get her arms through the sleeves! It was very annoying and frustrating for all of us carers. She knew exactly what to do not to get the coat on, then she would sit back close her eyes to pretend she was asleep; indicating she was not yet ready to go home.

I came to learn that most of the clients, especially the elderly needed a short nap after a heavy meal and moving them or playing loud music to those with good hearing senses was quite an inconvenience to them. Most of them appeared tired and worn out during most afternoons and behaved paranoid some days. Some enjoyed dancing after lunch and ' a nice cup of tea'. A cup of tea always restored friendship when things had gone wrong!

CHAPTER 5

Are Women More Prone to the Disease Than Men?

The months that followed, I tried to observe and collect as much information as I could, about my client and about the types of symptoms observed in other clients and their behaviours; compared to what I had seen. I wanted to see also how my client reacted under different environments.

I came to learn that there were times of clear manifestation of the symptoms of the illness in some clients but the same symptoms were less or none at all other clients. Others would show the same symptoms only at certain times of the day, other times no one would suspect anything was wrong with them. This was very puzzling. It was hard to establish what the real symptoms of the disease were. Everyday I tried to understand and carry out more research through observations on my client and other clients I came across. I read more books, reports, attended courses and meetings about the disease but the more I read about the disease, the more I became more confused. The symptoms changed daily and sometimes hourly. These symptoms were different in different clients; it was not only the weirdness nature of behaviour that was common but appearing confused and becoming forgetful. Some just stayed dumb, not talking to anybody, others talked lots, others were always very agitated, others over friendly. Sometimes some would ask me who I was. At one time after studying me for a while; one of the clients asked me "Are you a man?" I bust out with laughter, but later I realised, she could have been right to ask; because I had trimmed my hair short like most men. I was dressed in trousers too.

It was a nice day, the sky was blue; lined with a few strata little white clouds; It was brightly shining outside, despite the cold speedy winds.

Kevinah seemed very happy. She led me by the hand, "Come!" She beaconed me and I willingly followed her.

She led me to a room that was located at the end of the main corridor.

The smoking room. The air in there was hazy, filled with heavy smelly tobacco fumes.

There were people seated and smoking at a remote corner.

I felt like choking at the entrance, the thick fumes of tobacco had filled the room! I tried to resist, pulled back and I begged Kevinah not to get into the room, but she pulled me harder and managed to pull me inside. Sometimes Kevinah was stronger than me. She was tall and strongly built. I could not stop her so I faked a false sneeze and a cough.

"Gish, hee!" "Cocho! Cocho!" "This room makes me sneeze! I protested.

She turned, gazed at me and smiled but did not turn back. She continued, ventured into the room..

"Who is that?" A coarse lady's voice called from inside.

I tried to pull Kevinah back but she resisted. Instead, she lightly parted my right shoulder as if she was calming my coughing down! The voice came again, "Who is that coming in here? There is no space!" The same lady's voice shouted!

It was certain we were not welcome in the room! "Let's go back my friend, this place is not very nice for us, let's go back to the hall and find nice magazines to read!" I insisted.

Kevinah smiled murmured something and turned back to follow me. She had understood the other clients were not happy with our presence. Kevinah understood people's moods. If somebody addressed her in a bad tune, she would adversely react back. When one greeted her in a friendly way, most times she would smile and reply, "Fine!" In a friendly way! At times when I was low, she would ask me, "Are you ok?" Her actions at times bewildered me. She would say the right word at the right time. At that time I would wonder whether she suffered any medical condition as

alleged by other people! But times came when I was certain she had a

medical condition that needed treatment.

Just as we entered the Hall, Janet walked in pushing a trolley carrying cups and tea pots.

"Hello! Kevinah, here is a cup of tea for you!" Janet teased her as she poured tea in the cups.

Kevinah smiled, gave a light pat on one of Janet's arms; went passed by her and picked one of the cups containing the just poured hot tea off the trolley! Then picked a saucer and walked off with the tea in one hand and the saucer in the other.

The tea was steaming hot and unsafe for Kevinah to handle. Janet and I, exchanged glances, but we had to handle the situation wisely. Any attempt to take the cup from her would result in scalds, perhaps a worse accident! It would be a serious crime of neglect of duty and would end in disciplinary action against both of us- the staff!

For several moments both of us watched Kevinah in despair! Both our hands clenched on our mouths and eyes goggled like in a Suffolk Owl! We stood in restricted reserved silence.

For moments there was an unusual silence in the room. It seemed

Everybody was aware of what was happening!

Kevinah, oblivious of what other people's feelings were; continued her journey, found a low table, put the cup of tea safely on it and sat down comfortably on a chair next to the table. She then carefully put the saucer next to the cup.

When she had safely settled down; Janet and I, eyed each other in disbelief and consequently heaved sighs of relief! But not for long....

After a little rest, Kevinah got up, walked around, found another chair; but she did not sit down. She walked around the chair and pulled it aside. She then walked back to the trolley grabbed a side plate with two 'rich- tea' biscuits and transferred her latest find to the table where she had left her tea.

Before siting down, she picked a biscuit broke it into two halves, dipped one half in the tea and started to eat it. Then folded and held the other piece in the other hand!

She pulled the chair she had sat on earlier and sat down to have her tea.

"It was hard to work out what was going on in her brain. Sometimes, you might think she is not aware of what she is doing, but you later realise she just needed time to adjust, collect and translate the information into action or set it right before acting!" I pondered loudly.

"It is true!" Janet seemed to have entirely agreed with me.

Day after day, while at the Centre, I watched with concern the different clients affected by the disease and their behaviour during different times at the Centre. I was horrified how widely the disease had spread. There were clients from all races, nationalities, ethnic groups, religious differences and lifestyles. But I noted most of the members who attended the Centre were quite elderly, most of them in their eighties others in nineties and they were mostly women and fewer men. Unfortunately, on certain days, I sadly noted that some clients came with bruises on different parts of their bodies: their limbs, faces even on their bellies. Some came dressed in dirty clothing, some seemed not to have had a shower for days! At times there emanated a bad smell in the room.

On certain days, the staff had to give some clients a shower, change their clothes and wash their dirty clothes too. Each client had to bring a spare pair of clothing, and sanitary wear. We had to carry out personal care. My client was always very clean. Her family cared for her very well. They dressed her well and comfortably. She would walk in with a new dress and matching comfortable shoes and when commended on what she wore, she would be very happy and would afford a smile. She loved materials with colourful patterns; she would touch and examine the patterns and at times tried to pull at them as if to take the pattern out. But most of all, she cared to be clean. She was very private too. She never allowed anybody she wasn't sure of to undress her or do any personal care on her.

Some clients had to be cared for like babies. Some of them lived on their own and depended on carers who visited them daily but sometimes never turned up!

"It is part of nature, sometimes circumstances don't allow! Sometimes, the carers were paid to spend only fifteen minutes with the client!"

"What could the carers do in such a short time with somebody who takes ages to understand one word?" Miss Panessa amused us on one of those good days when we shared lunch break together.

Most of the clients who attended this Centre lived in their own homes and were looked after by their own children, spouses or hired carers. Most of them appeared health, and most times happy despite their illness. Kevinah always inspected her surroundings whenever she was dropped off both at home and at the Centre. She would then sit down; perhaps when she was satisfied everything was ok.

Each day I worked at the Centre I made and recorded my observations. I had to count the number of women and men attending the Centre and recorded the numbers; I realised there were more women than men in daily attendance recorded. For example:

DATE	DAY OF THE WEEK	FEMALES	MALES	COMMENT/ AGE RANGE 50-97yrs. /TOTAL DAILY ATTENDANCE
11/3/14	Tuesday	14	1	15
12/3/14	Wednesday	7	3	10
13/3/14	Thursday	8	0	8
17/3/14	Monday	14	1	15
18/3/14	Tuesday	14	4	18
19/3/14	Wednesday	8	1	9
21/3/14	Friday	11	1	12
24/3/14	Monday	12	1	13
25/3/14	Tuesday	14	1	15
26/3/14	Wednesday	14	4	18
27/3/14	Thursday	11	1	12
28/3/14	Friday	8	0	8
31/3/14	Monday	14	1	15
TOTAL RECORDED FOR MARCH 2013		**149**	**19**	**168**
1/4/14	Tuesday	14	1	15
2/4/14	Wednesday	7	5	12
3/4/14	Thursday	13	1	14
4/4/14	Friday	8	1	9
7/4/14	Monday	10	2	12
8/4/14	Tuesday	8	5	13
9/4/14	Wednesday	6	3	9
10/4/14	Thursday	6	5	11
11/4/14	Friday	5	2	7
14/4/14	Monday	12	2	14
15/4/14	Tuesday	8	5	13
16/4/14	Wednesday	6	2	8
17/4/14	Thursday	8	3	11
18/4/14	Friday	7	5	12
22/4/14	Tuesday	7	5	12
23/4/14	Wednesday	5	4	9
24/4/14	Thursday	6	2	8
25/4/14	Friday	8	1	9
28/4/14	Monday	11	4	15
29/4/14	Tuesday	8	4	12
30/4/14	Wednesday	8	3	11

Total recorded for April 2014		170	66	236
1/5/14	Thursday	6	2	8
2/5/14	Friday	8	2	10
12/5/14	Monday	13	1	14
13/5/14	Tuesday	8	3	11
14/5/14	Wednesday	8	2	10
15/5/14	Thursday	9	4	13
16/5/14	Friday	9	1	10
19/5/14	Monday	15	2	17
20/5/14	Tuesday	8	3	11
21/5/14	Wednesday	7	4	11
22/5/14	Thursday	8	5	13
23/5/14	Friday	8	1	9
27/5/14	Tuesday	7	3	10
Total recorded for May 2014		114	33	147
1/6/14	Monday	13	1	14
16/6/14	Monday	12	1	13
17/06/14	Tuesday	3	6	9
Total recorded in June 2014		28	8	36

Some days I did not attend the Centre, some days the Centre was closed.

Other days I became too busy and forgot to record. Some days some clients failed to turn up, some were not well, others had hospital appointment, sometimes they had been taken into respite ;at times there were sad news!

So and so had passed away over the weekend!

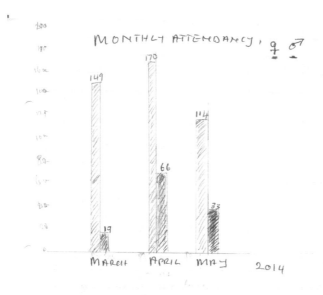

"May be women have to put up with more stress than men." Deborah one of the staff concluded emphasizing 'stress' as the major cause of the disease..

"May be men die off in the earlier stages of the disease, and women

tend to cope longer than men." I observed.

"Did you say women are more stressed than men?" Perhaps you are right!" But I have read in some research papers that most men who get the disease have had a brain injury earlier in their life while working or doing some sort of sport like boxing, football or have had a car accident, or indulged in excessive alcoholic drink; but what triggers the disease in women?" Counter interacted Janet.

"Oh! That may require some more research, but some women have a drinking problem too!" Both of us consented in chorus.

We urged and talked about the puzzling symptoms of the disease every day while we worked and cared for our clients.

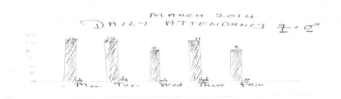

CHAPTER 6

The Disease, Types of the Disease and Symptoms

By 2013, the menace of the disease that had engulfed the world and devastated especially the elderly citizens had been diagnosed and given a Name- 'Dementia'. Some politicians dammed the disease the 'plague of the 21st Century'.

Researchers now describe the disease in various ways. The most common type of the disease is Alzheimer's.

You will be surprised; the disease has been in existence for a very long time. Most people, however, believed the symptoms were part of aging until the same symptoms were identified among the young!

At the time of writing this book, an intensive research into the causes of the disease had began; campaigns to raise funding for research and support of victims; training of carers and relatives of the victims on how to cope with the disease are already in progress.

The illness, however, has been perceived differently in different countries. Most people think the symptoms displayed by victims are part of aging. Others label it a kind of madness.

The illness is raising concerns, and there are fears among many countries that we may not have grandparents with sound minds in the near future.

Today, scientists describe 'dementia' as a set of symptoms which include loss of memory, mood changes, and problems with communication and reasoning.

These symptoms occur when the brain is damaged by certain diseases, including Alzheimer's, and Vascular dementia which is caused by a series of small strokes.

The condition is progressive, which means the symptoms will gradually get worse.

When people become aware of these difficulties they react in different ways. These difficulties vary in

For instance: Memory loss that disrupts daily life, forgetting recently learned information, important dates or events; asking the same question over and over again or needing to rely on memory aids such as reminder notes or electric devices for things that a person used to handle on their own. Sometimes forgetting names or appointments but remembering them later. Challenges in planning or solving problems for instance with a familiar recipe, difficulty in completing a familiar task for example driving to a family location; trouble understanding images. Confusion with time or places.

In advancing courses, the victim starts to have problems with words in speaking or writing; Misplacing things or loses the ability to retrace steps.

The person may start to withdraw from work or social activities, gets mood swings personality; display decreased or poor judgment or decision making.

When people become aware of difficulties, they react in different ways. The difficulties vary in thinking, remembering and reasoning.

The victims become angry, frustrated and try to cover up a problem.

The condition is progressive, which means the symptoms will gradually get worse.

In other ways, 'Dementia' is further described as a general term for a decline in mental ability severe enough to interfere with daily life; may affect memory, thinking, problem solving, concentration and perception.

Mild Cognitive Impairments

Mild Cognitive Impairment (MID) is a relatively recent term, used to describe people who have some problems with their memory but do not actually have dementia.

Korsako's Syndrome

Korsakoff's syndrome is a brain disorder that is usually associated with heavy drinking over a long period. Although it is not strictly speaking a

Dementia syndrome; people with the condition experience loss of short term memory.

Rarer causes of dementia

There are many other causes of dementia including **progressive supra-nuclear palsy and Binswanger's disease.** People with **Multiple Screrosis, motor neurone disease, Parkinson's disease and Huntington's disease** can also be at an increased risk of developing dementia (Facts sheet: Rarer causes of dementia).

There are over 100 types of the disease but the commonest established known are:

Alzheimer's disease-

This is the most common cause of dementia and is a progressive form of dementia characterised by loss of short-term memory, deterioration of behaviour and skills of language, intellectual, visual, spatial skills and difficulty with judgment.

During the course of the disease, the chemistry and structure of the

brain change, leading to the death of brain cells.

The changes that occur in the brain are: Loss of brain cells; Shrinkage of brain tissue, Presence of neurofibrillary tangles and amyloidal plagues causing brain cells to die. Changes affect cells in all areas of the brain, so a range of difficulties could be experienced.

People with cognitive symptoms associated with the development of Alzheimer's might experience depression, sleep problems and behavioural changes before showing signs of memory loss.

The latest study has found that people who developed cognitive problems that indicated oncoming dementia are more than twice as likely to have symptoms of depression sooner than those without cognitive problems. *(Jan.14,2015-Health Day news)*.

Scientists say that other behaviour and mood symptoms such as apathy, anxiety and appetite changes and irritability also arrive sooner in those who develop typical Alzheimer's symptoms.

Dr. Keith Fargo, director of Scientific Programmes and outreach Alzheimer's Association, USA, explains that what people need to know about Alzheimer's is that **it's not just problems with thinking and memory. "It is a universally fatal brain disease where you lose the cells in your brain over time and that it can manifesto in many different ways.** One way is through dementia, but it can manifest in other ways such as depression, anxiety, or troubled sleeping. "She narrates,

Vascular Dementia

The second most common form of dementia is vascular dementia. To be healthy and function properly, the brain cells need a good supply of blood. If the vascular system within the brain is damaged and blood cannot reach the brain cells, the cells will eventually die. This means that the blood supply to the brain is impaired, depriving the brain of oxygen causing damage(Infarct).This could lead to the onset of Vascular dementia-The most common cause is a stroke(blood clot or blood in an artery preventing blood flow.*(Lecture notes by Sonya Barns SPD-Training,2013)*.

Multi-infarct dementia (MID) is another form of vascular dementia and occurs when the individual experiences a series of 'mini strokes', which although would be barely detected; has an accumulative effect on areas of the brain deprived of oxygen. Most likely this was the condition which my client Kevinah suffered.

Dementia Syndrome or 'mixed dementia'

This is a condition where Alzheimer's disease and Vascular dementia occurs together. Symptoms are similar to either Alzheimer's disease or vascular dementia or a combination of the two.

Dementia with Lewy Bodies (DLB)

Lewy bodies are abnormal proteins that are thought to cause brain cells to die. Lewy body deposits are found in the cerebellum and occipital lobe, affecting balance and causing hallucinations. DLB symptoms are similar to those of Parkinson's disease.

Symptoms in people with DLB vary from day today, with levels of abilities inconsistent. Individuals also experience periods of lucidity which can lead to depression.

This can be very difficult for supporters to understand.

Fronto- temporal (Pick's disease)

A rare form of dementia, which damages the frontal and temporal areas of the brain. It tends to affect people at slightly a younger age (between 40- 65). Damage is usually focused in the front part of the brain. The individual may experience extreme mood swings, changes in individual personality and behaviour; although memory is not affected in the early stages.

At the time of writing this book there are over 18,000 diagnosed younger people with dementia in the United Kingdom. Young people with dementia require different services because they are more likely to be in work at the time of diagnosis, have dependant children; have financial commitments; have a rarer form of dementia: find it difficult losing skills at a young age and find it difficult to access support.*(March 2006 -Dementia Awareness Course Notes-First Response Training)*.

HIV_ associated dementia

Dementia due to HIV infection is caused by the HIV virus, though it is not known how it damages brain cells. It is becoming less common with the use of antiretroviral therapy. Behaviour, thinking and memory are affected. Symptoms include forgetfulness, poor concentration, difficulty in learning new things, confusion, changes in behaviour, and problems with balance and muscle weakness.

Huntington's disease (HD)

An inherited degenerative brain disease affecting the brain as well as the body affecting younger people (between 30-50) and dementia usually occurs. An abnormal protein is produced which is thought to cause destruction of neurons. Most of the damage occurs in the basal ganglia, which controls movement, but also other areas of the brain are affected, affecting thinking, memory and perception.

Creutzfeldt-Jacob Disease (CJD)

A Type of prion disease, which affects a form of protein found in the central nervous system and cause dementia by forming clusters in the brain, destroying brain cells and forming holes (Spongiosis).

Symptoms usually progress very rapidly, from minor memory losses and mood changes progressing to clumsiness, slurred speech and jerky movements. The individual eventually loses the ability to move or speak; loses bowel and bladder control and is unaware of their surroundings.

I was determined to make more observations and read more about the disease in order to help out my client. Unfortunately, I soon discovered there was very little I could do other than doing what was required and instructed by the Centre and by Kevinah's relatives in the care plan. So I tried to follow the instructions given to me, but sometimes it didn't work!

Symptoms changed too swiftly, it appeared, every day was a new chapter, the disease behaved like a chameleon. Every day was different! Kevinah would behave normal, have walks happily and have her meals well, but on the way to go back home she would change into somebody else! Wouldn't accept put on her coat or shoes and would not allow to be moved!

But from what I had read and gathered from the care plan I was now able to identify what type of dementia my client suffered. I ascertained she was really ill, despite her courage to walk, play and smile.

I had learnt my client had another condition - Diabetes type 2.

From the reports I had read Scientists had discovered that Type 2 diabetes may shrink the brain: People with Type 2 diabetes may lose more brain volume than expected as they aged. In diabetes, the disease affects in two ways:-damage to the blood vessels and damage to brain cells.

"How about memory loss?" I kept wondering.

Scientific Information indicated there are three different parts of the brain involved in memory and ability to process information; the fore brain, midbrain and hind brain.

The process can be affected by the three stages required to remember

Information: Registering the information, storing it and retrieving it.

I had to know more about the structure of the brain. To understand the

three stages I recorded the following information:

The brain: consists of the brain stem: which sits beneath the cerebrum in front of the cerebellum. The stem connects the brain to the spinal cord and controls automatic functions such as breathing, digestion, heart rate and blood pressure.

The brain is nourished by a network of blood vessels.

The wrinkled surface of the brain is a specialised outer layer of the cerebrum-the cortex.

Scientists have mapped the cortex by identifying areas sharply linked to certain functions: interpret sensations from your body: sights, sounds, smells. Generate thoughts, solve problems; make plans; form and store memories; control voluntary movements.

Scientists say the left side of the brain controls the right side of the body movements and vice-versa.

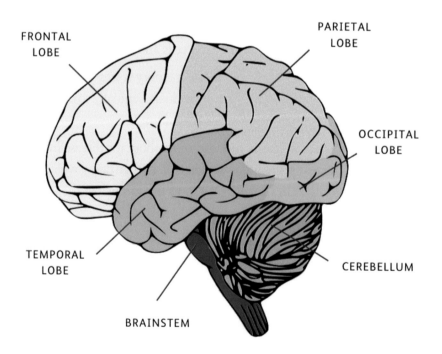

Parts of the brain

Adult brain contains 100 billion nerve cells and branches that connect at more than 100 trillion points known as **neuron forest. Signals** travelling through the neuron forest form the basis for **memories, thoughts and feelings.**

Cell signaling neurons are the chief type of cells destroyed by Alzheimer's disease. Signals that form memories and thoughts move through an individual nerve cell as a tiny electric charge.

Nerve cells connect to one another at **Synapses.** When a charge reaches a synapse, it may trigger release of tiny bursts of chemicals called **neurotransmitters.** These travel across the synapses carrying signals to the other cell synapse.

Alzheimer's disease disrupts both the way electrical charges travel within cells and the activity of neurotransmitters.

Signal coding

The brain has 100 billion nerve cells, 100 trillion synapses, dozens of neurotransmitters to make your brain's raw material and to code our thoughts, memories, skills and senses of who we are.

The Positive Emission (PET) scan on the left side of the brain reveals typical patterns of brain activity associated with: reading, hearing words, thinking about words, saying words. Specific activities pattern change throughout life as we meet new people, new experiences and acquire new Skills.

Healthy brain   advanced Alzheimer's

The patterns change also when Alzheimer's disease or related disorder disrupts nerve cells and their connections to another.

Alzheimer's disease leads to nerve cell death and tissue loss throughout the brain. Over time the brain shrinks dramatically, affecting all its functions. The cortex shrivels up damaging areas involved in thinking, planning and remembering. Shrinkage is especially severe in the hippo campus -an area of the cortex responsible in formation of new memories.

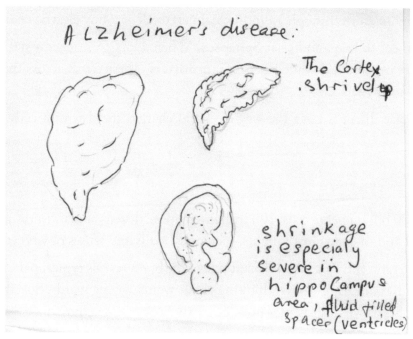

Ventricles (Fluid filled spaces in the brain) grow larger.

Synapses

Alzheimer's affected brain tissue may have fewer nerve cells and Synapses than a healthy brain.

Plagues- These are abnormal clusters of protein fragments which build up between nerve cells. Dead and dying nerve cells contain tangles which are made up of twisted strands of another protein that forms in the spaces between nerve cells. **Plaques** form when protein pieces called **Beta- Amyloid BAY_tuh AMuh-Loyd)** clump together. The beta-amyloid is produced when a larger protein referred to as the amyloid precursor protein (APP) is broken down. APP is composed of 771 amino acids and is cleaved by two enzymes to produce beta-amyloid. The large protein is first cut by beta secretase and then by gamma secretase, producing beta-amyloid pieces that may be made up of 38,40 or 42 amino acids. Research has shown that Beta-amyloid cause toxic damage to nerve cells. Another theory is that the

Beta-amyloid forms tiny holes in neural membranes which lead to unregulated influx of calcium that can cause neuronal death.

These abnormally configured proteins are thought to play a central role in Alzheimer's disease. The amyloid plaques first develop in the areas of the brain concerned with memory and other cognitive functions.(23 Aug 2018 https://www.news-medical.net.)

Scientists are not yet certain what causes cell death and tissue loss in the Alzheimer's brain, but **plaques and tangles** are prime suspects.

The small clumps may block cell to cell signaling out **synapses.** They may also activate immune system cells that trigger inflammation and devour disabled cells.

Tangles are formed by collapsed tau, or a protein responsible for keeping strands short in infected brain collapse into twisted strands called tangles.

Amyloid plaques form one of the two defining features of Alzheimer's disease, the other being **neurofibrillary tangles. Beta -amyloid** is also suspected to be responsible for the formation of the tangles, which also damage neurons and cause the symptoms of dementia. These are the defining proof of dementia.

When the tracks fall apart and disintegrate, nutrients and other essential supplies can no longer travel through the cells which eventually die.

Plaques and tangles tend to spread through the cortex in a productive pattern as the disease progresses. The rate of progression varies greatly.. It is reported that people with Alzheimer's have an average time of 8 years to live with the disease but some may survive up to 20 years. Changes may begin 20 years or more before diagnosis; mild to moderate Alzheimer's stages may last 2 to 10 years; in severe Alzheimer's 1-5 years.

The Earliest Stages

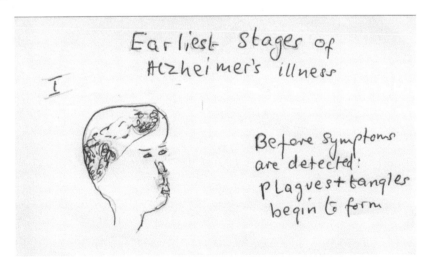

Before symptoms can be detected, plagues and tangles begin to form in the brain in areas involved with **Learning and Memory and Thinking and Planning.**

In mild to moderate stages:

Brain regions important to memory and thinking and planning develop more tangles and plagues. Individuals develop problems with memory or thinking serious enough to interfere with work or social life. The affected person gets confused and get troubled with money or expressing themselves or organizing themselves.

Plagues and tangles spread to areas of speech and understanding. The individuals may experience changes in personality and behaviour and may have trouble in recognising relatives, family and friends.

Progression through the brain:

II

mid to moderate
Stages:
More plaquest
tangles in thinking
memory - affect
work + social life
- change in
Personality
behaviour

Alzheimer's
PROGRESSION THROUGH
BRAIN

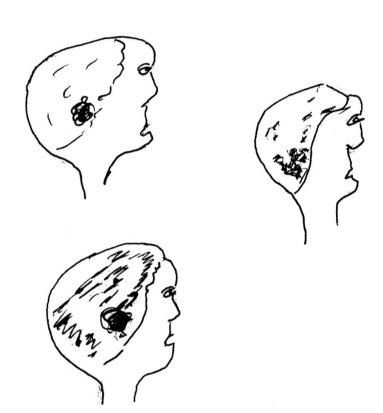

pLaques + tangles tend to
spread through the cortex in a
predictable pattern as Alzheimer's
disease progresses.

In severe Alzheimer's most of the cortex is seriously damaged, the brain shrinks dramatically due to wide spread cell deaths.

Individuals lose their communication; fail to recognise loved ones and to care for themselves.

In early stages: there is decline in recent memory, loss in the ability to take the initiative or plan. The person gets mood swings; Have difficulties in making themselves understood; and there is a tendency to loose interest in social skills.

During my work at the Samaritans Centre, I observed that there were some clients who preferred to be on their own and those who fancied to mix with only a particular group of people all the time and would not sit with others.

In the later stages of illness, sometimes referred to as moderate dementia, there is reduced ability to carry out tasks of daily living, there are sleep problems and loss of appetite.

When I met Kevinah she was reported to have sleepless nights; she would spend most of the day time sleeping on the coach.

In some people as the illness progresses behaviour of the victim becomes offensive or is hurtful, constant repetition when talking and inability to recognise things, even people.

Time came when my client couldn't recognise her own daughters, but recognised the one she lived with. However, at times the daughter had to explain herself before she could be accepted.

The Medical Scientists have recorded signs and Symptoms of dementia as follows:

The patients become confused, tearful, depressed, aggressive, incontinent, deteriorate in cognitive thinking; may behave sexually inappropriately; they are irritable, easily agitated. Disturbed sleep and forgetfulness is not uncommon among them.

It took me months to understand the course of the disease which was affecting my client. I tried very hard to learn her likes and dislikes, her reactions to different environments; despite the fact that we had by then become good friends and we could communicate effectively using a few words and body language. I could read and understand her moods and reactions. There were times Kevinah would become restless and would walk away, tried to open doors when she needed to go to the toilet. She had lost most of her ability to speak but at times could say a few words. She would pace the floors, try to gaze through glass doors, would try to open or unlock doors but at times could not utter a word or say: "Take me or show me 'the ladies place'.

Her temperament would change; she would become agitated and very restless whenever she needed to release herself. I came to understand my client's predicament. Thereafter, every time she became restless; I led her to the toilet, observed her after the toilet. After the Personal Care, she would always become calm, easier to handle, more pleasant and chatty.

Then I developed a programme to take her to the toilet at regular times and it worked. I observed that Kevinah would also become restless when she was hungry or thirsty or felt sleepy. I would give her a drink or something to eat. A biscuit, a glass of water or a cup of tea were always a good treat. After which we would go for a walk, hand in hand like real friends.

At one time, I noted Kevinah took longer than usual trying to pass her stool. Those days she would groan and make all sorts of mourning reactions. I suspected my client might have a problem of constipation or some sort of abdomen pain. I decided to report the matter to my supervisor and to her daughter whom Kevinah lived with. Later reported the incidence to the Centre manager .They all became very concerned; took the matter urgently and we supplemented her meals with fruits and vegetables and drinking water. I was advised to give her more water to drink than tea. Kevinah improved tremendously, she was happy to get to the toilet; she would sing and sometimes tap her feet on the floor instead of mourning. Kevinah's daughter also added more fruits and vegetables to her meals and asked me to give her water instead of tea. We all worked as a team and it worked! Kevinah showed good improvement, she would sing, laugh and mimic conversations.

There were times when Kevinah tried to get to the lavatory by herself, but could not find the entrance to the lady's room. I could sense her frustration! She could not talk to me, or tell me what she wanted; instead she would become very agitated. This was hard to understand and cope with at first and to give her the care she needed. Most times dementia victims are misunderstood when they react unpleasantly and may suffer considerably for a very long time without any help; at the same time causing frustration and desperation to those caring for them too.

CHAPTER 7

Environmental Influence

It was a cold day, the sky overcast with grey clouds; it had been raining most of the morning. The ground outside was wet; the atmosphere in the hall was dark and very dull too.

"Can someone tell me where I am?" Shouted Christina as she walked along the corridor that led into the hall. Most of the time Christina kept to herself. She mostly talked only to a pair of budgies kept in the cage in the hall and sat secluded at a particular corner near those birds. Her temperament had deteriorated lately. She was very rude to most of the staff and other clients.

Naomi one of the clients was strolling along the corridor.. She was searching for the entrance to the ladies toilet. She held her red hand bag clenched around her wrist she asked Christina:

"Where is the toilet?"

"You've just passed the door to the toilet are you blind?" Christina rudely answered her.

"I was just asking! You don't have to be rude!" Naomi begged pardon as she opened the door leading to the women's room and banged it shut.

Both women had just come in to attend the Day Care Centre.

Inside the hall, those who had come in earlier were having a cup of tea. Kathleen who had been furtively searching for something from her

Handbag begged for more sugar to sweeten her tea. "May I have some more sugar in my tea, please?"

A few minutes later, she was using her comb to stir the sugar in her tea!

"I think they never have enough sugar to go round for everybody in here; leave alone teaspoons!" She complained as she stirred her tea with a plastic comb handle, pulling her face, appearing very disappointed.

Meanwhile, a gentleman client, Bernard walked to the door, where I was standing.

"Can you show me the way out! I am late for my appointment; I should have left one hour ago! Just show me the way out! And call me a cub; I will buy you a drink!" Bernard asked and promised me a drink as he tried to open the door leading to the corridor. Obviously he was trying to escape from the Hall.

Meanwhile, as I attended to the gentleman, another lady client came along;

"You are the best of them all! When I see you I cannot be unhappy, I will buy you some food when you come and see me tonight, are you coming with me? Please don't let me down!" Allen, who was always happy to see me, begged as she approached.

"Please don't let me down!" She pleaded with me, shading tears.

"Oh! Hello! Allen, how are you this morning!" I greeted her as I locked the door so that Bernard who had promised to buy me a drink could not escape.

Suddenly, I remembered I had to attend to Kevinah. As I turned to get back into the hall to find her, I overheard somebody shouting:

"What is she doing over there? Leave it alone! We don't do things like

that here!!" It was Kathleen shouting at Kevinah.

Kevinah was of a different skin colour, from Kathleen. Kathleen always took the responsibility to correct, teach and show anyone to do things the right way; especially those whom she thought came from a different or lower social class. She apparently did not get along with most foreigners..

She always showed others where to sit, how to use folks, spoons,

and napkins at the dinning -'table manners' to be precise. What and what not

to eat. She would also shout at the staff who presented what she felt were 'boring' activities.

"I have been coming here for years! We never did something so

boring!" "Disgusting!" Kathleen would sneer!

"I have been coming here for years! I just told you we don't like listening to that kind of music!" she was at times exquisite.

Some days when in her best mood, she would put on the sweetest smile and say:

"Hello! Darling, how are you today? My mum always told me to greet people in the morning, have my teeth brushed before my breakfast. I always had my uniform ready and school bag packed the night before!" She would go reminiscent.

One hot afternoon, one lady client by the name Zipola appeared to be feeling hot, she was sweating and she kept fanning herself with a piece of paper. She struggled to remove the light sweater she was wearing, but her hands seemed stiff and stuck; she could not fold her limbs.

She tried to say something, but I was not able to understand what she was saying. The lady spoke in a language that sounded Chinese Mandarin, or one of the Far Eastern languages. I could see the lady was strugling to remove the sweater she was wearing.

She kept pulling it off! She tried to fish for the left sleeve but she failed! She dropped her hands in frustration. She tried again to pull the sweater off, and then pulled the sleeve again without success!

I had been watching the lady for a while, I felt her frustration too! I decided to help her out. I proceeded to her and located the right parts of the cardigan and I pulled the sweater off her.

While I attended to the lady, I did not realise one of the male staff wearing grey coloured goggles, standing in a far corner, was watching and was against what I was doing. He was aware I had been cautioned by Miss Panessa not to care for other clients. As soon as I finished helping Zipola put off the sweater, the watching man rushed towards us and burst out:

"You should never do that; you have no insurance, to touch her!"

I was struck by the man's rude remarks. I stood up and peered at him furiously. I thought I had never seen somebody so ugly. The man's face grew uglier as he watched me angrily; his eyes swaying from side to side

in the eclipsed coloured spectacles. I did not move, I moved nearer to Zipola. He uttered something in the same language I had heard Zipola speak. I noted they were either related or simply came from the same country.

"Watch your tongue, I did not do anything wrong! What type of insurance are you talking about?" "You are not doing your work otherwise you should have rushed in to help her when she needed help!" I shouted back pointing a finger in his face.

"You were told not to interfere with other clients! You are a one to one only to one client, understand?" he retorted as he regained his stand.

I felt like charging at him, but something inside me held me back! I

had to behave like a lady especially in the presence of the clients. For moments, I stood still, my hands clenched and trembling!

Then suddenly, I felt a gentle cold hand folding on my left clenched hand, "Thank you! Thank you!"

It was Zipola, thanking me, with tears trickling down her drawn eyes!

"You are welcome, Zipola, have a lovely afternoon. I responded and quickly left to find Kevinah, leaving the goggled-eyed man standing still like a statue.

On certain good days, I received verbal medals from the clients!

"You deserve a medal! I mean it! You do so much for us! We are very lucky people, free transport, you attend to us!" One of the clients applauded us on the bus as we escorted her home.

The lady had been coming to the Centre for over a year. She was a very alert and pleasant woman. She was a chain smoker; at that time she was smoking electronic cigarettes. She was quite small in body size, and advanced in age perhaps in nineties but moved very steadily without support and was of pleasant countenance, always smiling and very polite when she spoke.

"You are very patient! I see how much you struggle with that lady!" She commented as I helped my client, Kevinah to get on the coach to get home.

"Thank you very much for the complement!" I acknowledged, in

Appreciation.

"I really mean it!" The lady assured me.

'They must have misdiagnosed her, it must be a mistake, this lady has no trace of the illness!' I pondered quietly.

It was one afternoon; the clients had just had their lunch, one client, known as July got up. I could sense she needed to go somewhere or she wanted something done for her! She picked her green nylon coat. It was a valuable asset to her by the way she held and examined it.

I decided to take time and wait to see whether one of my colleagues would come to the lady's aid! None came.

July looked at me questionably as if saying: "don't you see that I need some help?"

I watched her in silence for a while. No other member of staff was nearby and perhaps none would ever come to help. I stood still for some minutes, not knowing what to do and then I decided to move.

'This time, I will have to let them know they have a responsibility to work with their clients, that's what they are paid for!' I grumbled rather loudly.

"If I helped, they would accuse me of taking over their jobs!" I

whispered to myself..

I had not forgotten the nasty rebuke I had received from the male staff the previous day.

I burst out! "Can someone come to this lady's aid?"

After a minute's silence; Miss Panessa shouted back, "We can see her, we shall help her around!"

Suddenly, one of the lady staffs, Janet, ran towards July.

"What's the matter July? Do you want to go to the toilet? She asked her. "No! I was just wondering, whether my tax cub has come to take me

home! Besides, I don't know where I am!" The lady started crying.

I left and decided to take Kevinah for a walk, leaving Janet attending to July.

As we strolled along the corridors we came across a gentleman who was one of the clients walking half naked, only with a top on plus the underwear but his trousers were missing! The man walked majestically, across the corridor, opened a door opposite us, got into the quiet room and sat there all alone.

As we came towards the end of the corridor, we overheard people talking in the staff room.

I opened the door and reported the incident of the naked gentleman.

"Oh my God, do you mean he is really naked?" One of them sounded surprised.

"Stuck naked! "I amused. "I imagine he thinks he is in his own bedroom, what a pity!"

Maria, one of the staff followed him up; helped put his trousers on, and I overheard him politely thanking her "Thank you!"

"I should have known he wasn't in his right mind!" I felt guilty for not

helping the gentleman earlier.

It is not uncommon that carers do fail to help a client when help is urgently needed; could it be due to the amount of pressure at work or is it negligence of duty?

It was very unpleasant weather; it had rained heavily earlier, there were still traces of cold wind blowing through. During bad weather, one had to be very careful when handling the clients; any form of restraint would be treated with contempt.

Kevinah came in, very quietly and sat down without saying a word.

She usually had lots to tell but this day, she openly told me off," Leave me alone! Now go on! Go!" she commanded me.

I tried to talk to her politely, but she ignored me. I asked her if she would fancy a warm cup of tea, or a biscuits, she did not pick any, she walked off instead.

I tried to hold her hand, she quickly pulled it away. I could feel her hands were cold and stiff.

Behaviour of a dementia victim can be very confusing; but a repeated pattern of behaviour can reveal a meaningful pattern of the

victim's needs that can help design a beneficial care plan.

Whenever, the weather was bad, or when somebody had mistreated her, Kevinah would always become stubborn, never allowed anybody in her way! She hated being controlled; you could see it on her face! She would physically reject any advance towards her. She would brush off any one who tried to distract her from going anywhere or picking anything she wanted.

On certain days, Kevinah would be brought in late to the Centre due to transport problems. She enjoyed the ride on the bus but if she sat on the bus for too long or was picked late from the house, later than she was used to; she would react negatively especially when getting her off the bus. She would pretend she was asleep, sometimes she knew how to resist getting up; She would hold tightly on the bars of the bus and would not move. At times when I wasn't there to pick her from the bus and she had to be left there waiting until I arrived, Kevinah would get agitated and would become difficult to any advances to move her. Change in conditions used to upset and agitate her and would become difficult to handle.

"Let her go or sit where she wants or prefers" Miss Panessa would instruct whenever she noticed any carer restraining a client.

At the same time, she herself, at times would fall in the same trap with a client, wondering through the kitchen corridors. She would close the door, and shout:

"Oh! No! Not that way!" she would shout at the client closing the door behind and pulling the client back.

Philip a new client and Kevinah both loved to wonder and would break free whenever they fancied a walk through the corridors.

Philip never resisted, when asked not to go to restricted places, but Kevinah sometimes resisted any attempts to stop her doing what she desired to do; to the extent of asking you "Why do you follow me for?" she would ask shaking her head disapprovingly.

Every day the two friends would attempt to do the same things, it did not matter how many times you would try to stop them.

On one occasion, I realised Kevinah was hungry; we had been on a long walk out.

As I warmed her food she sat patiently waiting for her food. She appeared very happy and would say, "Thank you!". "You are very welcome." I would respond.

I was very much touched by Kevinah's politeness. At the same time I was very happy she could still understand it was food that I am serving her.

Whenever, we got home after the day at the Centre, Kevinah had to be seated down by a low side table, before I could get to the kitchen to warm her food. Kevinah seemed to understand that she wasn't allowed in the kitchen. Most times she would sit still in the living room until her food was served. But at times she would follow me when I took a stride to the kitchen. She always wanted to help or do some work in the kitchen. She loved to wash dishes, tried cut the onions or carry her food to the dining room, especially when I took long to chop up her food into smaller pieces while in the kitchen.

When eating, Kevinah could use the knife and folk, but preferred to use bear hands, and I would always make sure her hands were clean before I sat her down to eat her food.

She was never allowed to come to the kitchen by her daughter because she 'would upset everything in the kitchen thinking she was tiding up' her daughter said. Sometimes the kettle was on and hot! Sometimes the cooker was hot! There were always fresh eggs kept nearby and Kevinah loved touching anything round-shaped-eggs, oranges and onions in particular.

My client was very well looked after by her family. Her daughter always made sure her mother had the best and balanced diet. Kevinah loved fish, chicken and rice most. Her meals never missed good meat, vegetables and rice. But on certain days it was drama when she fancied using the spoon and folk.

She would use the spoon ok, at first scooping the rice or sauce or vegetables.

Sometimes she would hold both the spoon and folk together, put them aside, and then eat with bear hands, picking the rice grains, one by one between her thumb and first finger. Sometimes she would use the other hand to store some rice grains and pieces of meat. She would later use the stored pieces to feed her; babies' (two doles she kept on the sofa). I would find pieces of rice and meat beside her dolls when clearing the table and floor after feeding time. At times Kevinah would litter the floor with whatever food pieces she didn't want to eat. At the same time, she would try tide up every time when food dropped on the floor and when she finished having her meal. She would wipe her hands clean with a tissue; unfortunately at times she would try to eat it. Sometimes she would put an empty spoon in the mouth, and begin to chew it; picking the food with her fingers instead, like a toddler would do.

Her daughters dressed their Mum in the most beautiful and comfortable linen. Bought her the best and most comfortable shoes. Kevinah was a lady of high style and expensive taste.. When she was dressed in good clothes, she would show off that she was dressed well, and when praised for her smartness, she would smile sweetly. She would show that she was happy. Most of the day she would behave pleasantly, and was easy to handle. Her positive behaviour would reflect she had been given a choice to choose what she wanted.

I observed that good weather conditions like sunshine changed my client's mood. She was happier and easier to deal with during warm and bright good weather. Cold, cloudy and wet days depressed her. Kevinah would be dull, moody, quite irritable most of the day or would be reserved and sleepy most of the day.

A recent report from research scientists from the University of Edinburg, UK, found that **Environmental Air Pollution** is a predisposing factor for Dementia illness. (28th July 2022-LBC Radio conversations, 2.30pn).

Kevinah, loved dolls, she kept and played with them like they were her real children; she gave then several kisses and would talk to them as if they were real human babies. Sometime they got smacked when she thought they were misbehaving.

She however, had this peculiar behaviour after her meals.

Always after her meal, she would try to remove a piece of pattern or a drawing decoration on the side table. It was a beautiful pattern that stood out like a piece of flower. She always tried to pick the same piece of picture off the table after her meal.

"It cannot come out, it is part of the table" I would try to stop her, but Kevinah would just laugh and continue to pull the piece off! She did that everyday after her meal! It was like, she was saying:

"One day I am gonna get you off this table!"

I later learnt, picking out patterns or conspicuous patterns from a surface was one of the symptoms of dementia.

Kevinah, had developed another habit, she loved to look through the windows to see the garden. Both at home and at the Centre. She stood at the same positions inside the house near the windows or doors in order to have a view of the garden. She never missed a day without looking through the window at the same position.

She had another strict pattern of behaviour. She would start her walks in the building both at home and at the Centre everyday as soon as she came in. She would inspect the Hall, change magazines from one place to another. Move chairs and cushions from one place to another. She would even move some tables. When asked why she moved them; she would murmur something, although her speech ability had been impaired; sometimes she

would speak clearly. We noted she was trying to make order of the place and we only intervened when we noticed she was in danger.

Sometimes, Kevinah cared for me. She would show concern when I was not feeling well!

"Are you ok?" Kevinah asked me one time when she caught me dozing off on a hot afternoon.

Sometimes she would not find the correct words to say; but she would murmur something or part me on my shoulder.

She would always arrange things when back to the house; put everything in order before she finally sat down. She did the same at the Centre, on arrival. She had that sense of managing, spotty cleanliness and command of orderliness before she settled down.

When I was told my services were no longer needed at the Centre, I remained with my client at home when she was brought home from the Centre till her daughter came home from work. I had become very fond of Kevinah. I had developed a very deep apathy for her, probably gone unprofessional. I treated her like my own mother and was worried how Kevinah was coping at the Centre without my assistance. I knew the Centre staff had more clients at times than they could handle and Kevinah needed a one to one; but there it was a decision made perhaps to save money.

A year later, Kevinah's condition deteriorated, she started losing weight, looked older and weaker. She lost balance and never managed to go for walks as she used to. Her ability to speak slowed down.

I observed Kevinah for some months when she was dropped at home. She was most times very disturbed, very aggressive most of the time very difficult to handle. It took her several minutes to calm and settle down when she got off the bus home. It was the same bad reactions during the hot summer and cold winters, and when she felt sleepy or hot. .At times she was very aggressive when she come back wet; desperate to go to toilet. It was never easy to force Kevinah go to toilet unless one was well versed with her ways! She was a very private lady and maintained her dignity even at toilet. She never wetted herself unless she was not led to the toilet at the right time.

Whenever I sensed Kevinah was upset, I would first lead her for walks outside, we would go round the shops when weather was warm, Kevinah would calm down. After her meal we would watch television programs. Kevinah loved interactive programs like Come and Dine with Me, Antiques under the Hammer, and she enjoyed cartoons like The Simpson's, as well as listening to News bulletins.

She loved cracking jokes with people, especially men she was used to in particular. At times she would try to chat with men presenters on television, joked with men workers who came to do repairs at the Centre. She chose among the staff whom to joke with. She would give friendly smacks when she felt one was naughty but only to the people she was used to and liked.

Working with Kevinah made me make certain conclusions:

That when one is affected with dementia, one is no fool; it is just that one may not be able to translate her thoughts into words that quickly for people to understand.

In order to make people understand her, the victim who may have lost speech ability, tries to devise means to express her or his needs; usually resorts to using body language in order to communicate.

Kevinah was strong willed and a devoted Christian. She would ask for help from Jesus and God most times crying out audibly, "Jesus have mercy!" "Oh! God Help me!" "God Have mercy!" Were frequent Kevinah's cries whenever she was tired and appeared confused. Very often when she had episodes of confusion she would cry out to God, Kevinah would recover and then regain her senses! Then she would shake her head and say, "Oh! My God! What am I doing here?" or "What is happening to me?"

I would put a hand around her and say to her, "You will be fine, let's go and have a walk."

Then Kevinah would smile, get up and we would go for a walk.

When I had to go for holiday; I had to leave my client under care of another staff hired by her daughter. When I came back Kevinah seemed to be happy to have me back. She seemed to have lots of stories to tell me, but had lost most of her ability to talk. I realised, she was getting older too. I could imagine she had missed me just as I had missed her. Most of all, I was very happy, she could recognise me after a month of absence.

Dorothy, another client at the Centre was another lady of habit; she always carried her knitting with her to the Centre, even though she never did any knitting at all. She would frantically look for her 'knitting' every time she was moved to a different place. When she was moved to do her

nails or to the dining table to have her meal; she would ask, "Has anybody seen my 'knitting' anywhere?" That time she would have left it behind on her seat or under the chair where she had been sitting. Perhaps she was concerned about it's safety.

Kathleen, was another one, she always carried a pair of bedroom slippers with her in a plastic bag, although she did not need to wear them at the Centre.

She would say, "My mum always told us to carry our slippers. We were never allowed to bring dirt in the house!" She would say, when she realised somebody was curious about her slippers.

Kathleen showed in every way a strict upbringing. She was very strict with the other clients. She would strictly observe and reproach anybody who misbehaved. She would always get into trouble with other clients who did not take her corrections lightly----

"That is not the way we hold spoons here!" "Sit properly, you silly cow!" Those were some of Kathleen's nasty reproaches.

So it was better, most times to make her sit with people who could tolerate her presence or simply move her to a different place. Better still, move the one she didn't agree with to a different group. That way, everyone would be at peace.

Philip, joined the Centre in the last stages of the illness, he had lost speech, could only repeatedly say two words. Food and water. At times he would stare blankly in one's face. But one could read the agony he was going through, his face expressed several lines in the forehead and he repeatedly brushed his right side of his face's fore front. He would walk around; communicated mostly by touch, or signs. He was quite friendly and a gentleman too; but other clients never coped with his extended friendliness. He would touch any part of somebody's body not knowing that some parts were private and most clients found it annoying. The waist, breasts, bottoms made women clients jump or scream.

He walked about gently, overturned cushions and books to steady them up or simply looked at them. He liked walking with Kevinah; sometimes they seemed to be discussing something together by looking at each other, or one bringing a cushion to another.

All dementia victims live in a different world of their own, which no one else can understand except themselves. .It is very difficult for someone else to understand this 'one's world' of desolation. Sometimes, the condition is mistaken to be a mixture of symptoms of the '**Locked in syndrome**',' **Depression**', '**Mental Illness' or simply damned bewitched**. It is very hard to tell people what one is going through when one has lost the words to say, when even one's loved ones cannot understand the long term gestures!

Let's talk to our elderly ones while they can still tell us their stories.

When they can still ask what they need and what they want!

CHAPTER 8

Institutions

One impending problem, however, is the failure by trusted carers to learn that the condition-'dementia' is an illness and not an aging process and medical physicians' failure to make an early diagnosis of the disease!

It is a mystery, misunderstood and there are lots of stereotypes about the disease.

The stigma caused by the disease has significant impact on the well- being of those who have been diagnosed with the disease and those around them. For those who care for the victims it is a daily trauma-a powerful shock that may have a long lasting effect!

Learning how to communicate with a dementia affected person is very difficult and at the same time communication is an important tool for both the victim and the carer.

People with dementia have a reduced ability to communicate; and because we people are different, communication problems differ from person to person.

There are problems with spoken words (**expressive dysphasia**); there is loss of the train of thought. This happens during the early stages of the disease. As the disease progresses speech makes less sense. The person loses ability to make complete sentences. Kevinah would surprisingly make complete sentences in her advanced stages of the disease: "I don't want to know!" She would say at times! One would wonder whether the answer was in context, answering the question asked! Most times she would answer using the same sentence when asked to go to toilet, or asked which way she meant to go. Sometimes she would say the same sentence when she was in a very confused state.

Victims with problems with sight, hearing problems, depression, or with physical problems with the production of speech (**Dysarthria**), suffer problems with communication.

There are considerations to adhere to when dealing with such problems to make life easier for both the carer and the victim:

It is important to avoid a negative attitude towards the victim; maintaining the person's personality which still exists and not condemning the person as a gone shell! He or she is still the same person you used to know!

Focusing on putting the person first, making the best use of what is remaining in that person you knew before the disease struck by reminding them of the best times you had; the places you loved to visit or visited (**Reminisce therapy**) and what they have achieved (**Reality orientation**).

When they behave what you think is outrageous-be understanding, don't be aggressive, be tolerant, respond appropriately with compassion and love.

There are Rights to protect the victims such as: The Mental Health Act 1983 and Guardianship that deals with people who are medically assessed as having a mental disorder (although Dementia illness is not a mental disorder), if the victims are thought to be at risk to themselves or others; a guardian can be appointed to make decisions on their behalf.

The Mental Capacity Act 2005-This act governs decision making on behalf of adults who lack mental capacity at some stage in their life, or where there has been an incapacitating condition since birth.. It covers all decisions, including: personal welfare, financial matters. Decision making by attorneys. Decision making by court appointed deputies.

Overburdening staff with too much work, paying the carers low salaries, employing managers who just sit on armed chairs flipping files and all the time answering emails and phone calls and never lend a hand to the staff, is disastrous to the wellbeing of the dementia victims.

All staff should work as a team for the good of the victims. Only those with compassion and love to care and look after these victims should ever take up the job.

Some countries such as Britain and USA, have some of the best well developed and equipped institutions with professional programs for caring for the vulnerable elderly and disabled people. The government has great concern for the elderly safety, health and wellbeing. There are set laws, rules and guidelines that govern all those working with residents and day care members..

At the time of writing this book, Britain boasts of a well organised care system employing over one point five million (1.5) adult social carers (Skills for care.org.uk 2021 census). Here most of the elderly people taken care of live in private or sheltered and nursing homes. Those who live independently in their own homes are offered full time care by carers who visit and offer services daily, as required by the individual.

There are several agencies, private and government institutions supporting the Government in employing carers to offer services to the elderly people in all private and Government Social services as well as private homes. There are problems within the institutions but there are policies and guidelines as well as rules put in place to follow to safeguard the victims.

It is not uncommon, although, to meet with daily and unique challenges at these institutions. One challenge is that there is never enough staff to handle the influx of clients. The available staffs are always pushed to their limits. Clients have a diverse and complex multitude of problems and conditions which even qualified physicians are not able to treat!

"Take that table somewhere else, after that make tea, then take that lady to toilet, then make the care plan. After which you will get their coats and escort them on to the coach to their homes! Make sure you do not mix up the respective house keys or codes!" Miss Panessa, a manager of one of the institutions would instruct one staff member.

"Please see that you do not leave her to wonder on her own" she would politely instruct me.

I rushed to find Kevinah seated in the corridor near the reception.

"Clients are not allowed to sit here! You must ask her to leave!" "Take her somewhere else or back to the hall!" The secretary at the reception ordered me one time.

"We have inspectors from the Care Commission, tomorrow, everybody must come on time and be friendly and smile to the clients. Keep the place tidy. Do not leave clients on their own!" Miss Panessa instructed in a meeting the day before inspection day!

In another corner inside the residential home, a resident victim begged a visiting relative:

"Please come and visit me more often, preferably during week days; weekends I am ok, the meals are nice. But other days they come with a menu; ask you what you would like, but they bring something quite different! But during weekends they know relatives are coming and will complain when they bring poor meals!" One resident lamented.

One summer day, when everyone was in high spirits, Kevinah, was invited to share a table with the other clients at lunch time.

"We must make her feel she is part of the Centre, she must learn to share her last days happily with others." One of the staff beckoned me to bring Kevinah to a table where six other ladies were seated.

As soon as she occupied her seat offered by the staff, the other clients broke into a dumbfounding chorus:

"Oh the negro-e.Yah! Yah! Yah! She must be hanged by the toes!" And they started laughing!

Poor Kevinah, carried on having her meal, because she perhaps couldn't make sense of what the song was all about.

One of the staff overheard the song and she quickly reprimanded the clients to stop singing. "It is not fair Olive, to sing such a song at the dining table! "She politely advised the ladies.

"Why not? It doesn't matter!" Another staff member, counter attacked.

Janet who was nearby, looked on and later came to tell me how sorry she was about the incident! I watched it all, this kind of racism unfolding even among the dementia victims.

"I always believed, hidden traits do exist in some people and they

show very distinctly when dementia bites!" Janet whispered to me. I agreed with her, and I put it on my next investigation agenda.

Sometimes, you might think, those who suffer dementia illness may not be aware of what they are doing or saying! But at times they are quite certain of what they are saying or doing! That is the most confusing and annoying part of it!

I remember during my first days at the Centre I was treated with contempt by some clients.

"I tried to clear up when the clients had had their tea and I got a ferocious attack from one lady client!"

"I say! Do not touch it!" "It's mine! Go away!" She shouted at me!

Then another time I tried to arrange tables for tea time, and I received the same vicious attack from the same client!

"Do not touch it! Leave it alone!" She shouted at me.

"It took me several months to be accepted and to comfortably sit next to some clients."

"It is dementia; the disease makes them over react." Janet explained. "But I never receive the same reactions from the other clients who also suffer the same illness!" I complained.

"Each person reacts differently to this disease, and the disease progresses through stages, each stage displays different symptoms in each victim, that is how complicated it is to understand!" Janet explained.

"What a shame!" "We must try to be very tolerant and compassionate to the victims, most times it may not be their fault when they behave unbecomingly!" I replied after a lengthy silence of ponder.

Several weeks passed by. It was a very cold morning. All clients came in complaining about the cold morning. I made and served tea to all the clients.

"Hey Janet, I gave an extra cup of tea to the lady who viciously reacted towards me when I was new to this Centre."

"Who was she?" Janet asked.

"The one in a red dress!" I pointed.

"Oh! I know, she is not usually very nice to most of us too!"

Janet admitted.

"This time she thanked me for that very nice cup of tea!" I amused.

From that day, the lady who had been unfriendly to me received me with a sweet smile whenever we met.

As we conversed, Miss Panessa, walked in.

"Hello! Everybody!"

"Justina, serve tea to the clients."

"Other staff, let's have a brief meeting," she announced.

I continued serving tea while other staff sat to deliberate about important matters regarding the Centre. "Am I not part of the staff of the Centre?' 'No! I am from another agency!" I reminded myself. "But I have been asked to serve tea to everybody not only to my 'one to one' client."

I served the tea any way to all clients as I had been instructed.

When the meeting started I could hear Miss Panessa was the only one speaking most of the time:

"First the Duty Rota, everybody must be involved."

"I need all books, all charts, music CDs removed from the shelves, walls and from corners. They want plenty of space for clients to move freely." Miss Panessa continued.

The meeting went on several hours.

Then Kathleen, the client who couldn't wait any longer snapped; "Why do we come here for? We sit here and nothing is going on!" What are they doing over there?" The impatient client commented as the staff held the meeting.

At the same time, members of staff sitting at the meeting appeared to be disgruntled. There were exchanges of unhappy whispers; displayed screwed mouths and some staff sitting with crouched backs!

After the meeting, some staff gathered in the staffroom. I overheard Janet whispering: "We shouldn't listen to her. She dominates all the talking!" "She should allow us to contribute some opinions too, why then meet?"

"You have to be careful, do not interrupt when she is talking!" warned her colleague called Joseph.

"Watch out she bites!" Deborah ranted.

"I don't care she should retire!" Janet retorted.

"I heard she is retiring soon!" Deborah confirmed.

"That is always her story! Then she better retire soon!"

Angry Janet summarised.

"Shss! Shush! Quiet! She's coming!" Deborah warned other staff, hearing the familiar sound of shoes rubbing against the tilled floor.

"Some clients need to be taken to the toilet!" Miss Panessa instructed

as she approached.

"I am not feeling very well today!" Joseph tried to excuse himself. "Then you shouldn't have come to work." Miss Pannesa was never compromising!

In such a challenging nature of work, one would have found Miss Panessa's treatment and response to the staff most appalling and insensitive.

The staff need motivation to help them to stay healthy, strong and active to work. If they are at cross roads with each other, the clients will suffer. The anger, anxiety and cruelty all is eventually spilled to the clients.

How workers understand each other goes far in developing the relationship between their work and how they deal with the clients. The ultimate goal is to serve and provide a healthy, peaceful and pleasant environment to everyone around them.

Training, entertainment and a word of encouragement are super doses for staff motivation and professional development.

In dementia care, it is necessary to stimulate the brain in both the career and the client.

Stimulation of the brain by playing one's favourite music; reminiscent, having breaks, even a treat with a sweet are quite helpful brain stimulants.

I found it very difficult to cope when I stayed with my client for more than six hours in a single day! Can you imagine what one goes through when you have to live with and care for a victim twenty-four hours each day in a year!

Tuesday was always a very hard day for the staff. Most clients had complex behaviour. There was this client who always wanted attention. She would ask the staff to take her to the toilet six times within the five hours she stayed at the Centre.

When delayed to be taken to the loo, she would scream:

"Are there no carers here?" "Why can't someone take me to the toilet?"

A carer would come rushing to attend to her.

On return from the toilet, while the staff searched for a suitable seat for her; as some clients would just occupy any vacant seat sometimes after a dancing spree; the lady would squeal like a piglet in the highest pitch:

"Where was I sitting? Please, take me out of this chair!"

"Please ask politely, if you need help" a member of staff would politely

answer back.

"I did say, 'please'. Lick your ass!" the vulgar impatient client used to answer abusively!

Meanwhile, whenever it was time to go home, another client would seclude herself into a corner away from others and was always determined not to wear her coat. She would slap anyone who tried to put it back on her.

"Let go off my hand!" She would shout if anybody tried to dress her up!

Meanwhile another client would always spend most time at the Centre walking about and when asked

why she didn't want to sit down she would reply:

"I am looking for my son. He said he would be back by now."

"Do not worry, your son will be at home as soon as we get there, but now just find a seat and enjoy your cup of tea till he comes!" A member of staff would kindly try to persuade her sit down to wait for her turn to be taken to the couch to get home..

"No I said I do not want the tea! I want my son!" The client would shout back with tears trickling down her chicks, her hand bag tightly gripped in her hands.

The day care Centre was part of a big complex. Three other units were used for residential clients. Sometimes the residents visited the day Centre on their own accord, and at other times were brought in to be entertained together with the Day Centre ones during big cerebrated events in the country.

St. Patrick's Day, St. George's day, Easter and Christmas days were always big cerebrated events. Other traditional events cerebrated were the Halloween festival and the Remembrance day during the month of November 11th.each year; where we all had to wear red poppies to commemorate respect for the officers who died while defending democracy.

The residential clients had each a self-contained room, a communal

Lounge and dining room. Although there was a central kitchen which supplied the whole complex, there were individual min kitchens attached to each unit. Clients were not allowed in the kitchen for safety and health reasons.

The complex offered residential respite care for those victims whose families who cared for them needed a break. The residents were helped to get up, have a shower and served meals. They had walks within the building, and were engaged in various activities which included indoor games, and entertained with parties and concerts. It sounded all very good and beneficial to the clients.

The building had a sensory room where they relaxed .In the sensory room was a slide projector, a music system, Chinese flicker and disco lights and comfortable sofas. The room was purposely used to relax and calm down agitated clients. I frequently visited this room with my client especially when she was agitated to calm her down.

Outside the building were beautiful gardens where the clients enjoyed fresh air and sensory essence from herbal plants and flowers. It was a perfect home for an invalid. The gardens were laced with green lawns; well cared for shrubs and seasonal flowers. A strong metallic fence interwoven with rare shrub species barricaded the premises from outsiders and kept the clients safe and permanently secured.

Each unit had a dinning, a lounge, and an office as well as good toilettes facilities. There was a fitted laundry department where residents' linen was laundered. Melodious music sound from speakers attached in all the expansive and long corridors. Passages with swinging and lockable doors which one had to know the key code in order to open them added security to the premises. Fortunately a minimal of the residents could learn the combinations, even if some keenly studied opening the door, they would forget the next minute. That way it was a very safe and secure premise that safely locked in all the residents.

One fateful morning a male resident, woke up dressed for a 'mission to accomplish.' I learnt from one staff member. The gentleman had tried for a week to escape and was seen trying the codes to open the doors, but the doors only beeped! That morning the smartly dressed elderly resident promised himself that he would prove to those unsuspecting carers who had kept him a prisoner all those years that he was no fool! He was going to show them he could find his way to the shops and buy himself a beer and a packet of cigarettes.

He dressed himself up smartly, had his breakfast and walked to the main door, stood there pretending to be reading the notices pinned on the walls.

He had noted some people came in through the door to visit some residents and noted the door opened to the outside. So he waited.

Soon a car pulled up outside, a young woman came out of the car and she quickly hurried to the entrance door, pressed a button and there was a buzz before the door clicked open. Before the visitor could step inside the opening door, the smartly dressed resident shuttled through the opening door, politely excusing himself.

"Please excuse me lady, I am late for my appointment", he addressed the visiting lady; who only smiled to acknowledge his politeness; and let him pass.

None of the staff noticed that some resident had escaped, until later in the evening when he did not turn up for a party where all residents had to be present.

They found him at the nearby bus stop waiting for a bus to take him home.

A nice hot cup of tea always made a big day to the clients. They would smile, talk over it and it seemed to bring them together ironing out their differences!

The music and dance kept them very happy and together too. Whenever music of the sixties and seventies was played they seemed to be very happy and they danced rigorously enjoying themselves.

Music of the likes: the petticoats; Elves Presley, Din Martin, Natkin Cole, Vera, Ricky Nelson, the Beatles, Ellen Sharpilow were some of their favourite artists and seemed to remind them of their youth.

The new comers however, had a rough time on their first days.

It was her first day at the Centre, she looked around, everything appeared new to her, an enormous room, strange people, strange voices, strange activities going on.

She appeared lost in a strange difficult world where she was no longer

in control. She kept touching her forehead, brushing her hair with her bear

hands, asking herself,

"Where am I?" She walked around scrutinizing the contents of the room.

"Where am I? How did I get to this place?" "I don't want to be here!" She cried as she studied the place.

"Everyone is new here, when is my husband coming? I want to get out of here!" She screamed.

"I have talked to your husband, he will be here soon! Now come and sit here with me and I will send a nice lady to bring you a cup of tea." Miss Panessa, the staff manager, comforted her.

"No thank you!" "I, say! I don't want to be here!" The new client continued to cry.

There were others who were simply naughty and playful!

At one time a voice came from behind:

"Hello, Nicky, How are you? Would you like a cup of tea? I am always hungry," the lady staff continued as she moved with the trolley .The clutter and rattle from the shaking cups and teapots filled the hall. She munched a biscuit as she talked to the clients.

"No, you are not hungry, you have worms! That is why you are always eating!" A lady client who was always naughty amused as she verbally attacked the staff member.

At another end Linda, another client seated next to one gentleman client recounted her school days how she used to walk two kilometers to the school. She narrated that she grew up in a care home, where nobody cared to cook breakfast early. She reported they had to do house work before their breakfast; which included scrubbing the floors with a brush and used a bucket to bring water.

"There were no detergents at that time. We used ash from wood and the floor shone spotless". Linda narrated.

"Oh! Thank you everybody. It has been a very nice day! It has been wonderful listening to you all! And if you do not mind, I wish to nominate the lady seated next to me to wind up the afternoon by thanking our esteemed speakers!" Daniel, the gentleman who was sitting next to Linda and a former lecturer at a London University who now had become a client at the Centre, politely applauded, turning to Linda.

A staff member clapped, and then all clients followed with uncoordinated claps

Jack, another male client sat gazing at the floor, he smiled when I

Approached him..

"Good morning Jack!" I greeted him, although it was past dinner time. He afforded a smile." Ok!"

Jack was one of those who never sat down when music was on. Now he sat comely but was trying to pull off the legs of a chair!

He kept fidgeting with his hands, and clapping even if there was no music in the back ground.

He was always attracted to anything conspicuous like colourful patterns in a piece of furniture such as drawings on a table, or carpet or pictures on the wall. He would even try pull at anything protruding from any surface. He would try to pull legs off the chair near him.

I soon realised there were many others behaving like this gentleman.

Most of them tended to pluck pictures and notices off the notice boards.

During one of the training sessions, I attended; I learnt that plucking things off the wall or from carpets was a common symptom among dementia victims.

"The condition makes them perceive things differently. "the tutor narrated. They see patterns in a carpet as if it is a reality." She said.

This is the saddest moment, seeing somebody going down, seeing things differently and another one shading tears! You wish you could care for that person, and be able to turn the clock back but you can't!

One client who was talkative and sociable to almost everyone suddenly started losing temper and was talking things you couldn't even imagine!

"You are all idiots, why do you keep coming to my house! I don't remember sending any invitation to any of you!" She would rattle off.

I soon learnt that most of the clients who attended the Centre had once

lived decent lives; had responsible jobs worked in big offices:

They were Doctors, midwives, nurses, cooks, professors; judges, teachers, models, musicians, gardeners. There were also those who lived different lifestyles: alcoholics, drug addicts to decent church goers!

My conclusion was that the illness did not even discriminate against age or gender; and was no particular person's disease, it would affect anybody!

Despite of all this understanding, most people still disparage the affected elderly with untold ridicule and rejection. They termed the victims pretenders, doing right things at times and intentionally doing wrong things in order to gain attention!

This is how little we understand the condition of dementia.

If for a healthy person, it proves difficult to communicate with a dementia victim, how much more would it be for a dementia victim to communicate with a healthy person who does not have a clue what it feels like to suffer from dementia!

Sometimes the victim struggles to say something but fails to find the right words to say it!

In order to communicate with my client, I had to look straight in her eyes and keenly studied her facial reactions.

She would sometimes make faces at me, when she thought I had acted foolishly.

Folding her nose and looking straight into my eyes lifting her thin lips ; she would tell me off when she thought I was in her way.

"I say, let me pass!" she would shout raising her voice and hand to show me, where she wanted to go.

I often received slaps when I interfered with her sleep.

Sometimes she would smile, and at times she would laugh her heart out! when I said something funny.

Keen observations of Kevinah's reactions and body language such as gestures and facial expressions helped me learn how best to communicate with her.

Kevinah loved music, and when she was happy would sing even while on the toilet seat; tapping her feet on the floor.

When she was at her highest peak of happiness she would agree to dance! But she preferred to sit and hum to the music and dance while seated.

I danced lots for her. She seemed to enjoy it very more when I riggled my big bottoms! Kevinah would laugh her heart out. I sometimes used dancing to please her, or brighten her mood up when she was low and moody.

Kevinah enjoyed being with nice people, she engaged in conversations when allowed to, although she would not find the right words to say, she would make gestures and murmur something. She was trying to participate in the conversation.

Her most troubled times were when she needed to go to toilet and she was not lead to the right place, She paced the floors, opened doors peeped through glass doors and windows. She would appear agitated when she couldn't find the entrance to where she needed to go.

When she felt sleepy and tired she would mourn sometimes, or walk away to find a quiet place to sit and rest. At that time, if disturbed or restrained prevented to get to wherever she wanted to go or sit she would get very cross with me to the extent try fighting or slapping me .I grew to understand her predicament, as I continued to work with her and tried not to cross her way, although there were times when I needed to be firm with her.

She was such a pleasant lady .Most times, she would give a light smack when she thought you had been naughty!. She loved company of men, smiled at them and teased them with facial expressions; she liked rolling eyes at them.

Kevinah had lost most of her speech before I started working with her, she regained some of the words back after a few months of care. I could hear some of the staff applauding her for having gained her speech. "Oh! she can now speak, she never used to say words so clearly!"

"How are you today?" she once greeted a stranger, a builder, who had come in to make repairs in the Centre. She would stand looking at strangers; the men working in the garden or children walking on the street and smile at them.

She liked talking to one of the drivers and a handyman who used to talk to her in her indigenous language. Both men belonged to her ethnic origin. Although she seemed to have lost the power of speech, Kevinah could still speak and understand very well two languages :English and her indigenous language.

It takes time to learn, handle and cope with a dementia victim, but with patience, compassion, and the will to help out somebody, one learns to cope. It is a noble job if you can make a difference in someone's life.

CHAPTER 9

The stigma of Living With the disease

For days, weeks and months, I tried to remember, if I had ever seen Any one in my home country behaving in the same way l had seen the Clients at the Centre behave…

Then I remembered during one of my holidays in my own home village, I paid a visit to one of my in-laws. Her mother greeted me and narrated strange stories to me. I wasn't sure the granny remembered whom I was.

"She never used to talk that much as far as I remember." I got concerned.

"She has gone insane lately, do not listen to her!" My sister in law

Advised me.

In another part of the same village, a widower who had lost his wife a few months earlier had gone on hunger strike!

"He was always wondering in the village, several times found strolling along busy traffic streets. "Sobbed his daughter, Dorothy who lived and cared for him.

One unfortunate day, he was found walking naked on the street eating from garbage bins.

"People say, he has ran mad! He could not cope with the loss of his wife." One of his neighbours whispered to me. "It's sad! He used to be a very proud man, unapproachable, but sometimes was very polite. He was a regular church goer; he never missed to go to church on Sundays!" Another elderly lady neighbour added.

People believed his death was associated with the loss of his wife; eating contaminated food and walking naked in the cold. But he had very caring children.

There are no established institutions in that country where the elderly can be taken care of. People there believe the elderly must be looked after by their families, but some people do not have families or known relatives. If he was aggressive they would have taken him to a mental hospital, but he was a very quiet man; only at times he would behave like a mad man. He was lucky he had a daughter who cared for him.

How many others with the same condition who are languishing in mental hospitals, suffering at the hands of those who should care for them but fail them because the condition is wrongly diagnosed.

In the same country, I remembered, my own late grandmother, who had turned in 100 years. She would invite strangers from the street and serve them with tea or food, told them all sorts of stories. She would tell them about her late husband as if he was still living, but the husband had passed away several years back. She could sing most Church Hymns without looking at the Hymn book. She got arthritis and could not walk, so we moved her to live with us and put her on a wheel chair. The frustration of not being able to move freely, the pain in her legs and not being able to invite friends developed stress on her brain and her reasoning became delusional.

"Who is that nice man who buys the nice food for me?" she asked me one day.

"He is your son in law grandma! My father" I answered her.

"How about the woman who prepares and brings in the food for me?"

Continued grandma.

"That is your daughter! My Mum, grandma!" " Have you forgotten her?" I reminded her.

"Oh it is a long time since I saw her last." She would wonder off.

I couldn't tell whether my granny forgot things due to advanced age since she was over 100 years of age; or was she another victim of Dementia?

I decided to search for more information on the current trends of the disease in different countries.

The information was overwhelming. The disease was wide spread but different countries regarded the cases interestingly different.

At the time of writing this book, in most African and Asian countries, people with dementia are stigmatized, marginalized and excluded from important and vital roles in society.

In Ghana, social exclusion is one of the consequences health officials have to deal with. It is devastating for both the victim and their families. In Uganda, people associate the illness with aging, others have a vernacular name: 'Kazoole' or 'confused fellow' for the condition. People segregate themselves from such families, no one fancy's to marry from such a family, when a family member is known to suffer from such a disease. People secretly talk about the victims and tend to avoid and exclude them from important social community roles.

In most African countries and other developing countries the disease is termed a kind of 'madness' or a 'result of witchcraft' and in most cases victims are simply left on their own to care for themselves.

In developed countries like USA and UK, significant research is going on and a breakthrough to control the disease is eminent.

In the Balkan states, there are few cases but of no great significance for reporting

"People say they might have eaten chemically poisoned food "Mr. Mackonis from Lithuania reported to me. "Others are said to have been born with brain injury and are kept in special hospitals" he continued.

Although, it is widely believed that in Africa, elderly people are well looked after by their children and sometimes relatives.;many do not have children and may not have willing relatives or resources to afford the cost of care. The victims of dementia are left on their own or cast out as social rejects. Governments in such countries need to borrow a leaf from the unreserved gestures of care from the developed countries and care for the elderly especially those who suffer long illnesses or terminal illness; irrespective of their social or family status.

Iam tempted to pass on a paper I read during my search for information about the disease: *'Unattended Dementia'* given to the British Psychology Society (1990) by Dr. Tom Kitwood, University of Bradford: perhaps it will help people who are insensitive, uncaring or neglectful to understand how it feels like to suffer the illness of dementia:

Dr, Tom Kitwood, writes of the hazy atmosphere of confusion the victim finds him/herself in, " *you cannot make out whether it is summer or winter, day or night.* He describes the declining cognitive **ability***: but just as you are beginning to get the picture, your knowledge slips away, and you are utterly confused...*

Dr.Tom Kitwood, talks about one of the symptoms of the loss of the recognition of familiar objects the victim of dementia referring to them as *"an impression of people rushing past you, chattering like baboons. You catch sight of a familiar face; but as you move towards the face it vanishes."*

The fear of carers and terming them oppressors....*"You are grabbed by people much stronger than yourself. Sometimes bundled in a van with others who seem to be equally miserable*

He describes reality of the disease as causing desperation and loss of hope: *"everything falling apart, nothing makes sense. You know it wasn't always like this....there is a clear memory of good times you knew where and how you were .... and when you were able to perform daily tasks with skill and grace."* A sense of oppression hangs over you, abandoned forever, left to rot and disintegrate into unbieng.*" **Dr.Tom Kitwood, University of Bradford :(British Psychology Society (1990).**

On a BBC television broadcast in London, Tom, a former track driver and now a victim of the disease, narrated how it started: "I became panicky, everything made me snappy! I remember I used to become angry at the till, at Sainsbury, when doing my shopping! I could not pack my shopping at the pace the lady was pricing them on the till!" he narrated.

"Many symptoms or signs are still undiagnosed." he lamented.

A doctor from China, on BBC, TV the next day confirmed that only 60% of the cases are diagnosed in UK, but in china,80% were not diagnosed.

"One person is infected in every 4 seconds in China." reported the doctor.

The next day, a UK news broadcast reported 44 million people infected.

Again on 19/6/2014, the British Health Minister,, announced:

"There is a need to fight the disease through concerted research, at the moment 44 million people are affected in Britain."

In January 2015,830 million people were reported affected by dementia related diseases in the United Kingdom.

On February 16,2015, A £30m war on Alzheimer's was the headline in

Daily Express paper "British scientists were to spearhead the search for the cure of dementia." Giles Sheldrick reported.

I recall the true encounter with a rich family man in my village back home in Africa, who fell sick and lived with a strange illness for a very long time before he died. People gossiped about him a lot that he used to wear his wife's half petticoats, that was what he preferred to dress up. Before he fell ill he was a prominent business man with two big families in different homes. He was polygamous family man. He kept several concubines too, most of them several years younger than himself. People accused the wife who lived with him a 'witch' with the strongest love charm, because he favoured and chose to live with her.

"The 'Love portion' made the man insane instead." one of the villagers amused.

I remember when I was a little girl, my mother sent me to deliver a message to the family and when the wife came to open the door, the husband came along following her like a small child. I remember seeing him dressed in a white half petticoat lined with a white lace. Then I remembered the stories about him wearing the petticoats! The man died several months after my visit.

In the East Indies Islands, those who show similar symptoms are

simply termed 'confused'.

In Philippines, when elderly people behave abnormally, it is part of aging.

In some Eastern European countries, it is a type of madness, known as Demenciya; others refer to the behavioural symptoms a sign of aging.

There are lots of myths and stereotyping about the disease. More is needed to create awareness to highlight the symptoms in order to reduce the stigma suffered by the victims and those living with them and have to care for them.

CHAPTER 10

Suspected Causes of Dementia

Months turned into years, I kept wondering why the scientists took so long to find a cure for this horrible disease which was wiping out mostly our elderly citizens. I searched for more information about the disease from the internet, and any literature I could find about suspected causes of the disease. One had to find the causative agents, get rid of them in order to remove the symptoms. Several theories were recorded by scientists and medical authorities.

During the 1960s, Aluminum was suspected to cause Alzheimer's disease. The suspicion led to concerns about everyday use of cooking pots, foil, beverage cans, anti-acids and ant-persipirants. Reports concluded that scientific studies had not yet confirmed the role for Aluminum in causing Alzheimer's.

Head injuries, Hydrocephalus,clinical depression, Downs's syndrome, vitamin deficiency, untreated high blood pressure, Creutsfeld Jacobs Disease(CJD);long period of excess alcohol intake,brain tumor, Parkinson's disease, Family history and HIV/Aids conditions have been suspected to cause dementia.

A study on brain injury in veterans indicated higher risk of developing dementia-Alzheimer's in their later years for the military veterans who suffered brain injuries during their service.

A report from the Neurology Journal showed 16% of the 180,000

Veterans aged 55 and above who had suffered head injuries developed the disease; a 60% increase compared to those veterans who had not suffered head injuries during their service.

The same report said that veterans who had multiple risk factors such as post -traumatic stress disorder, depression, or heart disease in addition to the head injury were more likely to develop dementia. The lead researcher, Debora Barnes, an epidemiologist at the University of California-San Francisco, Veterans Affairs Medical Centre, confirmed the records; however, she concluded that this did not mean that every simple person who has repeated traumatic brain injuries will develop dementia.

"It is not clear why head injuries may play a role in dementia, but it is possible that the more insults the brain experiences, the more vulnerable it becomes," counter signed Debora Barnes.

The Neurology Journal is however, skeptic about repeated blows in boxers and consequence development of the disease. Although boxers who suffer severe repeated blows to the head are at higher risk of dementia in old age, studies have been mixed about whether head trauma can lead to the mental decline in dementia..

In a related report on repeated blows and brain injury; an interview with a Dr.Mackie by BBC radio 4, on 3ʳᵈ.February, 2015.confirmed the post traumatic occurrence of dementia in sportsmen. Dr.Willy Stuart from Glasgow, Scotland reported of a 24% increase in retired footballers dying of dementia as a result of repeated concussions to the brain.

Ninety-eight percent (98%) of Footballers were reported to suffer brain injuries due to concussions and chemical imbalances symptoms. It was confirmed, Post concussions could lead to Dementia. British researchers urged for further research among rugby, footballers and boxers.

The study at the California Veterans Affairs Medical Centre stated that none of the veterans had dementia at the beginning of the study in 2000s, but by the end of the study, sixteen-percent (16%) of those who had suffered a serious head injury had been diagnosed with dementia, compared to only 10% of those without brain injury-a sixty-percent (60%) increase in those who had suffered head injuries.

Other researchers dispensed the occurrence of the disease in the kind of injuries that happen in everyday concussions on the soccer field.

Jeffrey Kutcher, a neurologist, a concussion expert and associate

Professor at the University of Michigan Health System in Ann Arbor, denied there was any evidence that those kind of milder injuries lead to later problems.

"Dementia is caused by a variety of factors including genetics, lifestyle and injuries"-he said.

There are risk genes with the strongest influence reported to cause the disease: The neurology journal reported.

The Apo lipoprotein (E-e4(APOE-E4).

Scientists estimate that APOE-E4 may be a factor in twenty to twenty- five (20-25) percent of Alzheimer's cases.

The APOE-E4 is one of the three common APOE genes the others are APOE-e2 and APOE-e3.It is reported that everyone inherits some form of APOE genes from each parent; but those who inherit APOE-e4 from one parent have increased risk of Alzheimer's and for those who inherit the gene from both parents are even at a higher risk -though not a certainty.

The APOE-e4 gene is reported to increase occurrence of Alzheimer's symptoms at a younger age than normal.

Deterministic genes:

Further reports indicate deterministic genes in families that when inherited will develop the disease. These are the Amyloid Precursor Protein (APP); Presenilin-1(PS-1) and Presenilin-2(PS-2).

The Amyloid Precursor Protein (APP) discovered in 1987 is the first gene with mutations found to cause an inherited form of Alzheimer's.

The Presenilin-1(PS-1) identified in 1993, is the second gene with mutations found to cause early onset of Alzheimer's.

Presenilin-2 (PS-2) discovered in 1993 is the other second gene discovered with mutants found to cause early onset of Alzheimer's.

When Alzheimer's disease is caused by these determinant variations, it is called "autosomal dominant Alzheimer's disease (ADAD) or Familial Alzheimer's disease and many family members in multiple generations are affected. Symptoms nearly always develop before the age of 60 and may appear as early as at 30 or 40s. Currently it accounts for less than 5% of cases. The Alzheimer's report continues.

In another report scientists insist the risk of Alzheimer's is increased by age and family history as well as heredity-

Other factors include the age after 65 years and that the risk doubles after age 85 reaching to 50%.

The risk is dramatised as we grow older.

At a conference in Copenhagen, 2014, reports indicated, rising number of the disease in the aging population.

In developed countries the numbers are tabled and are rising, while the numbers in the developing world is thought to be severely underestimated.

Dr.Keith Joseph, a doctor at the Mayo Clinic in Massachusetts general Hospital USA, reports of scans of 56 older people believed to be cognitively normal that showed tau build up in several brain regions correlated with memory loss.

.In another development, scientists reported of another protein (TDP- 43) different from amyloid and tau that make up brain tangles and plagues.

"From the 342 people in the study of the aging people all had amyloid plagues in the brain but many showed no dementia symptoms before they died," Dr.Keith Joseph the leader scientist reports.

"Out of the 342 participants, however, 195 or fifty-seven percent (57/%) had the abnormal protein (TDP-43) and less than 5-percent of the healthy general population would be expected to have the TDP-43 abnormal protein." continued the doctor.

"If there are 2 million people walking in America with Alzheimer's but they are not showing any symptoms of it, think of how major that is!" Dr.Keith Joseph, amused.

"If you have this protein (tau) you're guaranteed to have the symptoms- if you do not-you have a 20 -percent chance you won't show symptoms even though you have the disease as defined by amyloid in the brain!" Dr. Keith Joseph continued to the amusement of all the conference attendants.

The scientists reports above sight accumulation of abnormal proteins in the brain as the major cause of Dementia and concussion of the head that cause brain injury as one of the predisposing factors.

Recent Corporative Epidemiological studies at the University of Edniburg,in Scotland have found in Cardiac restraint, small dirty pollutants found their way into the brain through blood circulation consequently causing Dementia. The scientists concluded that pollutants in the environment are predisposing factors to Dementia!

Weaver birds devouring a palm tree of it's leaves; to build nests leaving the stem hanging for life!

An assimilation to: 'the plague of the 21st.Century'. Photograph by Louise P.N.Kibuuka at Entebbe Airport Uganda.

CHAPTER 11

The Scramble for the Cure!

At one of the international research centers Scientists struggled for Strategies for prevention:

Scientists from Massachusetts General Hospital in Boston USA claimed they had made a breakthrough:

In a news report of the International New York Times of Monday 13th, of October 2014; scientists reported of a latest research on how to study Alzheimer's disease and search for drugs to treat it. The scientific venture by scientists from Massachusetts General Hospital in Boston was led by Dr.Rudolph Tanzi, acting on a colleague's idea, Doo Yeon Kim. The idea was to use embryonic stem cells-the cells that could become any cell of the body- and grow them with a mixture of chemicals that made them into neurons.

"We have found a new approach that will provide complete prevention." "The new approach is to find mutant genes in order to find drugs to cure the disease." Suggested Doo Yeon Kim to his director, Dr.Rudolph Tanzi.

The International New York Times of October the 13th 2014 reported that the Massachusetts scientists gave the formed neurons Alzheimer's genes and grew them in wells in Petri dishes that were lined with a commercially available gel .Then they waited.

"Sure enough we saw plagues, real plagues", Dr. Tanzi is reported tohave said.

"We waited and then we saw tangles, actual tangles! It looks like you are looking at an Alzheimer's brain." Dr. Tanzi concluded.

The research agreed with George Glenner's Beta Amyloid protein accumulation in the brain making plagues and forming tangles that had been discovered earlier. The only hope was the discovery of drugs that could prevent formation of both plagues and tangles of which the combination proved fatal for brain cells and dementia sets in. Scientists said.

On Tuesday, March 3 2015, Chicago, Reuter's reprints.com reported the Scientists at Harvard University prevention trials studies about tau, Alzheimer's other protein:

For the first time Researchers at Harvard University, were scanning the brains of healthy patients for the presence of a hallmark protein called tau, which forms toxic tangles of nerve fibers associated with the fatal disease-Alzheimer's.

Early diagnostic signs were sighted as the first advance to find the cure.

In another development, the same journal reported that certain **biological changes in the retina and lens of the eye, and in the sense of smell might help predict w**hether people with no or minor memory issues may go on to develop Alzheimer's. This meant **Smell Test may help to detect Alzheimer's.**

The report confirmed that doctors believed it might be possible to detect early indicators of Alzheimer's by testing one's eyes and nose for build-up of a protein that causes Alzheimer's a type of dementia.

During a Copenhagen conference, in 2016, scientists concurred that **eye scans and sense of smell test** could be a useful affordable tool for early detection of dementia. Also they reported of a new abnormal protein linked to Alzheimer's that had a possible link between **sleep disorders** and onset of dementia.

Healthy habits slow the cellular signs of aging.

A report by Dennis Thompson, of July 29/2014 in The Healthy Day News reported of new research by Professor Eli Puterman of the University of California SanFransisco, School of Medicine. The Professor reported that **Healthy habits slowed the cellular signs of aging.** He stated that **exercise, healthy diet** and **quality sleep** could protect the body against stress, slow down the aging process at cellular level.

Globally one third of Alzheimer's disease is related to risk factors that can be potentially changed-such as lack of exercise and education-a report from the Lancert Neurology journal indicates.

The report explained that a sturdy of 100 older women who went through stressful events were linked to increase shortening of the telomeres- the protective caps at the ends of chromosomes that cause quick aging of cells.

Cellular aging has been associated with age-related illness such as Alzheimer's, cardiovascular disease and cancer. Telemeres are composed of DNA and protein and these protect the ends of chromosomes and keep them from unraveling.

Another latest diagnostic tool to test onset of dementia illness was the **pace diagnostic tool.** Researchers at the Albert Einstein College of medicine of Yeshiva University and Montefiore Medical Centre staged the new diagnostic tool:

The new study reported that the way older people walk may provide a clue about how well their brain is aging and could allow doctors to determine whether they are at risk of Alzheimer's disease.

Results showed that those whose walking pace begins to slow and who also have cognitive complaints are more likely to develop dementia within 12 years..

Genetic link was also sighted:

It was reported that those who have a parent, a brother or sister or a child with Alzheimer's were more likely to develop the disease. The risk is reported to increase if more than one family member has the illness. When the disease is found to run in families, is either heredity (genetics) or inheritance.

On 5/3/2015, the Health Day revealed that a brain protein tied to Alzheimer's was spotted in young adults.

Alan Mozes, a Health Day Reporter reported that brain plague build up long linked to the onset of Alzheimer's disease, had been identified by researchers in the brains of men and women as young as 20. The build up of abnormal protein "amyloid or plague" known to accumulate and surround specialised cells called neurons in seniors and those suffering from Alzheimer's was found in the **'basal forebrain cholinergic neuron"**--- researchers said, which was especially vulnerable to cell death among Alzheimer's patients. Such neurons are key to memory and attention.

The study co-author Changiz Geula, a researcher and Professor at the NorthWestern University Feinberg School of Medicine, Chicago, condemned "Amyloid as bad." However, she admitted, Scientists were not sure of the mechanism by which amyloid build up caused brain damage.

The report confirmed environmental factors or both may play a role.

"We don't know the exact mechanism by which it causes damage, or if amyloids build is the main trigger for Alzheimer's, so we can't say that it actually causes the disease. But for a long time we have known that it accumulates," Reaffirmed study co-author Changiz Geula.

"What is new here and very surprising is that we found an accumulation of this amyloid inside the nerve cells of individuals as young as 20" Geula added.

"What we need to do is look at larger number of elderly to see whether the ones who have more amyloid face a higher risk of Alzheimer's or poorer (thinking) abilities," she explained.

On a similar note, a striking a cautionary statement by Dr. Yvette Sheline, a professor of psychiatry, radiology and neurology at the University of Pennsylvania, Pereiman School of Medicine, who was not involved in the study highlighted the "complicated " nature of the findings.

"Nonetheless, it is interesting that amyloid accumulation could occur so early in the basal fore brain." She exclaimed!

Dr. Stephen Salloway, director of the Neurology, the Memory and Aging programme at Butler Hospital in Providence RI, agreed the findings would ultimately point to "a key step" in the beginning of Alzheimer's disease..

Alzheimer's disease a progressive brain disorder is the most common form of dementia among older people. It is estimated that 5 million Americans and over 1.4m British nationals have the disease, and that number is growing. (Health Day News for Healthier Living...05/03/2015 USA, and July 2022 Health Statistics UK).

On January 14th, 2015, the Health Day News reported a new study that revealed that people with cognitive symptoms associated with the development of Alzheimer's disease, a one type of dementia might experience depression, sleep problems and behavioural changes before showing signs of memory loss.

In the study, researchers found that participants who developed cognitive problems that indicated oncoming dementia were more than twice as likely to have symptoms of depression sooner than those without cognitive problems.

Other behaviour and mood symptoms such as apathy, anxiety, appetite changes and irritability also arrived sooner in participants who developed typical dementia symptoms.

"What people need to know about Alzheimer's is that it's not just problems with thinking and memory."

"It is a universally fatal brain disease where you lose the cells in your brain over time and that manifests in many different ways. One way is through dementia, but it can manifest in other ways such as depression, anxiety or troubled sleeping." Narrated Keith Fargo, director of Scientific Programmes and Outreach Alzheimer's Association.

One local gentleman, who lives in my neighbourhood, blamed the condition on chemical contamination of food in temperate countries. He insisted that people should only eat fruits and vegetables that are shared with weevils," That was his scientific test for purity from chemical poisoning that destroy the brain." He recommends that people should desist from using weed killers to root out weeds and turn to organic farming.

"The weed killer chemicals spread into crop fields contaminating food we harvest and eat! This is a factory of death!" He lamented. "People should insist on eating food that is organically grown, that is the only way we can ensure a balanced and safe diet that won't destroy our brain cells." he added.

This is an urgent call for research on the effect of weed killers on the human brain.

Is there any treatment?

Prevention has always been better than cure!

Prevention of Alzheimer's could be encouraged with cutting certainrisks like smoking and sitting in one place. Having lots of exercise and reducing obesity/overweight (ITV Good morning Britain, 15/7/2014)

Several organisations are setting strategies to combat the disease. The Alzheimer's Association's Research and New Investigation Research Grant Programme(NIRG);Dementia Care homes, Support Care and programs are some of Care organisations and companies set to support research for the cure and care for the victims of dementia.

On Tuesday, March 3 2015, Chicago, Reuter's reprints.com reported the Harvard prevention trials studies about tau, Alzheimer's other protein:

For the first time Researchers at Harvard were scanning the brains of healthy patients for the presence of a hallmark protein called tau, which forms toxic tangles of nerve fibres associated with the fatal disease- Alzheimer.

The new scans were part of Anti-Amyloid Treatment in Asymptomatic Alzheimer's or A4, the first designed to identify and treat patients in the earliest stages of Alzheimer's, before memory loss begins.

In a related incidence, the Association News reported of a study from Mayo Clinic to have identified a different toxic protein called tau as the likely cause of Alzheimer's.

Researchers planned to do tau imaging on up to 500 patients in the A4 trial.(Reuters.)

Dr.Keith Johnson, Director of Molecular neuro imaging at Massachusetts General, who was leading the imaging portion of A4 trial confirmed that: "Tau is the bad actor on the frontline that tears up the brain. Being able to see it in living humans is a breakthrough." he said.

Most researchers believe that tau and amyloid are connected and the A4 study has now been expanded to track the build-up of both in the brains of the patients on trial -the report continued.

Several studies and drug companies have developed drugs to remove amyloid from the brain in a bid to keep tau in check and alter the course of Alzheimer's but the drugs on trials have so far failed to show a significant benefit.

According to Dr.Reisa Sperling of Massachusetts General Hospital in Boston, who was leading the 1,000 -patient trials; tau is commonly found in small amounts in healthy people above the age of 70 years, but it is generally confined to one area of the brain called the **Medial Temporal lobe,** reports Reuter's reprints.com

In 2012, Eli Lilly's drug-**Solanezumab** was reported to have failed to slow the disease in patients with two trials of patients with mild to moderate symptoms. But combined results showed the drug appeared to slow cognitive decline by 34 percent among patients who started with only mild symptoms.

On March, 24, 2015, the Association of Alzheimer's bulletin reported that Dr. Reisa Sperling, a physician at the Harvard University and project director of the A4-study - reported that Clinical trials of **Solanezumab** could slow down or even prevent Alzheimer's disease.

Some positive results were reported for early stage drug trials. Clinical trials using aducanumab (B11B037, Biogen) were presented at the International Conference on Alzheimer's and Parkinson's disease in Nice, France.

The results were categorised as-1. Positive, Safety and Tolerability; reduction of Amyloid plagues in the brain and slowing of decline in memory and thinking abilities as well as function.

The trial was to clear amyloid plagues produced by a particular protein

(The report indicated amyloid PET scan was used.)March 20, 2015-Association of Alzheimer's News.)

There are drugs offered by physicians:

Antidepressant may help reduce beta-amyloid production. A common antidepressant, Citalopram (sold as **Celexa**) may cut production of beta- amyloid, a protein considered a chief cause of the disease.

A plea for more research

"The disease has been ignored for a long time, it is time to concentrate on research to tackle the killer disease now second to cancer, laments." the British Prime minister (BBC News 19/06/2014).

At the time of writing this piece of information, over £ 37 billion global funding is estimated to have been spent on research and treatment of the disease

Media has played a big role in support for research for the cure against Dementia illness.

On 8th July 2014,BBC News reported that Scientists had made a break through to diagnose dementia prone people at an earlier stage from a Neuroprotein presence in the victim's blood.

A Latest report from the Alzheimer's Association International highlighted a protein TDP-43 suspected to cause Alzheimer's disease. The protein previously linked to Lou Gehrig's disease and other brain diseases is now suspected to cause Alzheimer's disease. Dr. Anton Porsteinsson- University of Rochester School of medicine New York, reports.

More discoveries indicate a study of blood-based biomarkers linked to Alzheimer's. British researchers say they have identified 10 blood proteins associated with a high likelihood that people in this study with early signs of memory loss would progress to Alzheimer's disease dementia over the next year.

Experts caution, however, that while these preliminary results are encouraging, a blood test for Alzheimer's is not around the corner. According to the Lead Researcher-Simon Lovestone, Oxford University, Alzheimer's begins to affect the brain many years before patients are diagnosed with the disease (Alzheimer's and Dementias News-8/7/2014).

"How fast dementia progresses will depend on the individual person and what type of dementia they have and the action they take towards maintaining an active mind and body." The lead researcher adds.

Use of Gene Mutations Approach

In another development, new approaches to fight the disease lead by Dr. Friend and Dr. Schadt from the Icahn Institute, medical research institutes at Mount Sinai in New York are studying gene mutations in a bid to provide complete protection of family members against dementia.

They are studying a survivor of the Whitney family Mr. Dough Whitney whom they have set as exhibit A in the new approach in the search for helpful genetic mutations sought to develop drugs that can treat Dementia. Mr. Dough Whitney is the only survivor from a family of generations of sufferers wiped out by Alzheimer's disease.

The approach is similar to that was discovered and now being used in HIV and Cholesterol: preventing HIV from entering cells and reducing the amount of LDL cholesterol.

Both discoveries have led to drugs treating the diseases like Osteoporosis and Type 2 diabetes and Alzheimer's. (Alzheimer's Association News, Jan, 2015).

Trial Drugs (January 23rd.2015 Alzheimer's Association Report).

1. Drug treatment for high blood pressure Perindopril is being used in African Americans.
2. Use of safe doses of antibody to abnormal tau protein.
3. Using Biologically Active Dietary Polyphenol Preparations in pre diabetes and mild cognitive impairment (MCI) individuals.
4. Trial of possible substitute energy source (Oxaloacetate) for the brain in individuals with mild to moderate Alzheimer's.
5. A study of the effects of specific fats called -medium chain triglycerides(MCTs)efficiently converted into ketones in the body for memory improvement.

Latest fight to find new drug treatments for Dementia is spearheaded by a collaboration of British Scientists termed the Drug Discovery Alliance (The Daily Express of Monday February, 16th.2015. reports.)

According to Dr.Eric Karran, of the donor Alzheimer's Research UK, funding the alliance research, the venture is to tap innovations, creativity, ideas and flexibility from a coalition of academics, doctors and drug experts who will test new treatments at Oxford, Cambridge Universities and University College London. The first medications were expected by 2020.

The £30million five year project(Alliance Research) is a direct response to the desperate lack of effective treatments for those living with devastating brain diseases writes Giles Sheldrick of the UK Daily Express February 16/2015 .

According to the Daily Healthy (October 21, 2016, internet explorer. The recent results of a new Alzheimer's drug trial published in the journal Nature

Indicated that the drug **aducanumab**, had been hailed, as the first of its kind to remove the buildup of amyloid protein in the brain, believed to prevent brain cells communicating, leading to irreversible memory loss and cognitive decline.

The news went on to say several other Alzheimer's drugs had been designed to target the buildup of amyloid protein in the brain, but none had

Succeeded in clearing the protein and improving outcomes for patients in the final stages of previous clinical trials.

A total of 165 participants were given varying dosage levels of aducanumab, over a year as well as one group who received a placebo.

"The drug **aducanumab** is the long awaited and much needed breakthrough the mainstream has been waiting for." Reported the Daily Health News

The researcher is reported to have found that the highest dose of aducanumab resulted in an almost complete clearance of the amyloid plagues. Dr.Alfred Sandrock from the Massachusetts based biotic company Biogen, which is hoping to bring the drug to market hails the drug: "This is the best news that we have had in over 25 years and it brings new hope to this disease. The trials of treatment on patients are reported to have been done for over six months.

Over 400 drug trials recorded earlier, none of the drugs had been shown to combat the disease, reported the Daily Health.

The Daily Heath News hails the success of the **aducanumab** drug but cautions on its side effects.

Aducanumab has been reported to cause a condition termed ARIA characterised by leakage of fluid from the blood into the brain-a potential damage to the brain function.

On a Monday the 7th June 2021,Harry Johns: infor @alz.reported the approval of Aducanumab for the treatment of Alzheimer's disease, but not as a cure but for slow progression of the condition for those with mild cognitive impairment (MCI) due to Alzheimer's disease.

The demand for the cure is by far outstripping the supply; hence the **Inverse Proportion Curve!**

The scramble to find the cure for the illness; 'Dementia' continues!

Printed in the United States
by Baker & Taylor Publisher Services